WINTER'S CRIMES IO

WINTER'S CRIMES IO

Edited by Hilary Watson

ST. MARTIN'S
NEW YORK

Library of Congress Catalog Card Number: 78–60975

First published in the United States of America in 1979

ISBN: 0–312–88237–8

Contents

The stories are copyright respectively:

EDITOR'S NOTE

On its tenth birthday *Winter's Crimes* continues its tradition of publishing stories that have never before appeared in print, except possibly in America.

I would like to thank the twelve distinguished contributors for their various crimes which have created such an entertaining collection; and my special thanks go to George Hardinge for giving me the opportunity to undertake such an enjoyable task.

Hilary Watson

J. R. L. Anderson

THE BLACKBERRY PICKER

The driver of the Mini trod on everything and the car
slithered to a stop. Like many small cars whose owners
find that monthly salary cheques shrink horribly with
garage bills, its brakes were not adjusted as well as they
might have been, and it pulled over towards the ditch on
the nearside of the road. But the road was dry and it
didn't matter much. The girl tore off her seatbelt and
flung herself from the car. 'Oh God,' she said aloud to
herself, 'he seems to have been shot.'

She had been vaguely conscious of hearing a shot as
she drove along the quiet country road, but farmers were
often out after rabbits or the occasional pheasant, and
she had thought nothing of it. She was thinking primarily
of lunch, and wondering if there was enough left on the
weekend's half-shoulder of lamb to make a meal for her
father and herself. Jennifer Brill worked as a dispenser in
the chemist's shop in the small market town near the
village to which her father had retired. She was well-
qualified as a pharmacist and could almost certainly have
got a better job, but when her mother died there was no
one else to look after her father, and he so loved the
Downland countryside and his garden that it would have
been cruel to uproot him for Swindon, Oxford, Reading
or some other big town where better jobs would be. She
loved the country, too, and was content enough to jog
along, her job at least giving her enough for independence
and a secondhand car – subsidised by the fact that she
could share her father's cottage. There wasn't a lot of

money. Her father's pension was not inflation-proof, and went back to a time when managers of smallish tea plantations round Darjeeling owned by private companies didn't have lavish pensions, anyway. Her father, however, had planned for eventual retirement as far as he could, and the most sensible thing he had done was to buy the cottage they now lived in – worth a lot more than he had paid for it a quarter of a century ago, and with half an acre of garden, which kept him happily occupied and contributed quite a bit towards their living by providing most of the vegetables they ate. Jennifer did wonder sometimes what would happen when her father became too old for the work, but that wasn't yet. Thursday was her half-day, and she was looking forward to lunch at home and, after lunch, to a trip to Oxford to see if she could buy the kind of skirt she wanted at a sale.

Home, lunch and shopping were all gone from her thoughts now, and she was conscious only of the figure that seemed to have fallen out of the hedge into the ditch. As she ran up she saw that he was an elderly man, crumpled into the long grass, nettles, and trailers of briar that filled the ditch. He had fallen backwards, so that she could see his face. There was a neat small hole almost in the middle of his forehead, with blood, but not much blood, trickling from it. Jennifer had never seen a bullet wound, but consciously or unconsciously her mind related the man's injury to the shot she had heard and she knew at once that he had been shot. She also knew what he had been doing in the ditch. The thick hedge was rich with blackberries, and the man's left hand was still gripping the handle of a small basket, lined with newspaper that was purple-stained with blackberry juice. The basket was about one-quarter filled.

Jennifer's instinct was to try to drag the man out of the ditch, but she knew enough about First Aid to know that a badly injured person is usually best left as he is until skilled help can be brought. She ought, though, to make him as comfortable as she could before she went for help, but he seemed comfortable enough as he was. The sloping side of the ditch was almost like the back of a chair, and his head was resting gently on a tussock of the grass that disguised the fact that the ditch was a good three feet deep. Warmth – the late September sun still had warmth in it, but an injured body loses heat quickly and he ought to be covered with something. She had a rug in the car, and as she went to get it a man came running towards her from a gate that led through the hedge into the field behind it. The gate was about fifty yards down the road, and she was getting out the rug when the man came up. 'What on earth's happened?' he said. 'I thought I heard a fall behind the hedge, and then I saw you stop.'

'There was an old man picking blackberries, and he seems to have been shot,' Jennifer said. 'I saw him fall as I was driving. I'm just getting a rug to cover him before I go for help.'

'Good God . . . Good God . . . I wonder. . . . I was shooting rabbits in the field – it's my field – and I wonder if a bullet could possibly have ricocheted or something. What a dreadful, dreadful thing. Look, I'll wait here with the man, and you telephone for doctor, ambulance and police. There's a call-box in Spurbridge village – it's only about a quarter of a mile away. You can't miss the box because it's on the road, just at the corner of the village green.'

'I know it,' Jennifer said. 'I live at Linworth – that's the next village on this road, and I drive through Spurbridge every day.'

'Good. I think you should get off at once. I don't like the look of that poor chap in the ditch.'

Glad that there was someone else to keep an eye on the hurt man, Jennifer got back into her car. It took only a minute or so to get to the call-box, and she was thankful to find it empty. She dialled 999 and a quick voice asked what help she needed. 'I want a doctor and an ambulance and I suppose there ought to be police – there's a man been shot,' she said.

'Right, then I'll put you through to the police. They'll bring a doctor and an ambulance. Just stay where you are.'

Almost at once a police voice was on the line. It was the station sergeant at Marlborough, though Jennifer didn't know this at the time. 'What's the trouble?' he asked.

'I'm speaking from a phone-box at Spurbridge. I was driving towards Spurbridge – actually I'm going to Linworth, where I live – when I thought I heard a shot and I saw a man fall into a ditch. I think he'd been picking blackberries. He's very badly hurt, I think, and he wants help at once. I just covered him up with a rug from my car. There's another man with him, and he promised to wait while I telephoned you.'

'We'll get a doctor to you straight away, and I'll send out a call to the nearest radio car. The police car will probably come first. Can you wait at the Spurbridge call-box until it comes? Then you can show the officer exactly where the injured man is.'

'Of course I'll wait. Can I telephone my father while I'm waiting and tell him I'm going to be late in getting home? He'll be worried if I don't.'

'Certainly. Another officer has put out a radio call already. There's a car only a few miles from Spurbridge, and it's on its way now. You won't have to wait long. Can I have your own name and address, please, miss?'

Jennifer duly gave her name, rang off and telephoned her father. She'd barely put the phone down after talking to him when a police car pulled up outside the box. There was a man in police uniform at the wheel of the car, and another man dressed in an ordinary suit got out. 'I'm Detective Inspector George Rogers,' he said. 'I was on the way back from Swindon when we got a message that you'd telephoned about an accident.'

'You've come marvellously quickly,' Jennifer said. 'Yes, there's been a dreadful accident. Have you sent for a doctor?'

'That's been taken care of. He'll be along soon, but he has farther to come than we had. Can you take us to the accident?'

'If you'll follow my Mini we'll go back there at once.'

'If you don't mind, miss, can you come in the police car? Your car will be quite safe here, and if we're going to need an ambulance and a doctor the fewer cars on these narrow roads the better.'

Jennifer got in beside the driver and in a couple of moments she was pointing to a man standing by the roadside. 'That's the man who said he'd wait while I telephoned,' she said.

The inspector knelt beside the injured man, looking strangely peaceful lying back against the grass bank of the ditch, covered with Jennifer's car rug. 'I don't think a doctor can do anything for him,' the inspector said gently. 'But we'll leave him as he is until the doctor comes. Do you know who he is?'

'Yes, I do,' said the man who'd come from the field. 'He's old Jim Cartwright – lives in a cottage by the green in Spurbridge. Must be well into his seventies. Used to be a railwayman, but retired some years ago. He's a good general handyman, and he's done odd jobs for me from time to time.'

The inspector recognised the man who was speaking. 'You'll be Mr Henson – I'm sure I've seen you on the Bench,' he said.

'Yes, I am a magistrate. I farm most of the land round here. It's been a late harvest this year because of the poor summer, but a fine September's helped a lot, and we've just finished Pitt's Field – that's the name of the big field behind the hedge. There's always a lot of rabbits after we've cut, and I go after them to keep them down, pestilential things.'

'So you were shooting when Mr Cartwright was shot?'

'Yes. I don't like to think of it, but he could have been hit by a ricochet from one of my shots. If you come into the field I can show you exactly where I was – the dog's still there, with the rabbits I'd bagged so far, and my rifle beside them.'

Having asked Jennifer to wait with the constable-driver, Inspector Rogers walked with the farmer into the field. Mr Henson was rather more than a big farmer. He'd inherited Spurbridge Manor from a cousin, and in the days when such terms had any meaning – they still have some meaning in the countryside – he'd have been said to belong to a county family. He was now in his early fifties, automatically president of half a dozen local branches of national societies, and almost equally automatically a Justice of the Peace.

The inspector followed the magistrate into the field. The straw had been baled and taken away, and there was only stubble now, with a solitary late-surviving poppy making a stab of colour by the gate. It all seemed infinitely peaceful under the clear September sky, sunlight making the stubble look like thin bars of old gold. But death, and not alone in the still figure in the ditch, was there, too: a finely-bred Golden Retriever sat patiently guarding three dead rabbits. 'Topsy's the best gun-dog I've ever had,' Mr Henson said as they walked up. 'She's a mouth like silk – pick up a bird without disturbing a feather – and if I tell her to stay put she'll wait all day until I tell her she can move. Okay now, Topsy,' he went on; the dog got up, and came and stood protectively beside him.

The inspector looked at the rabbits, all killed cleanly with one shot. On the ground beside them lay the rifle, which Mr Henson had put down when he ran to see what had happened in the ditch. The rifle was a .22, an expensive weapon made for fine marksmanship, and fitted with telescopic sights. The inspector, who was a countryman, did not approve of going after rabbits with a .22 – it is sadly easy to wound and not to kill. He would have used a twelve-bore, with fairly heavy shot. 'Do you normally shoot rabbits with a .22?' he asked.

'Yes. I know what you're thinking, and I wouldn't

recommend it – wouldn't permit it on any land of mine –
for anyone who is not a first-class shot. I am a first-class
shot.'

'I take it you have a firearms certificate?'

'Of course.' Mr Henson seemed slightly nettled. 'May
I remind you that I am president of the North Wessex
Association of Rifle Clubs?' He recovered himself, and
added, 'Naturally you must do your duty, Inspector.'

'I don't doubt your certificate, sir, but I'm afraid I
shall have to ask you to produce it. That can wait until
you get back home. Since the man in the hedge – Mr
Cartwright, I think you said he was – appears to have
been shot we must find out if the bullet could possibly
have come from your rifle.'

'I've said already that I'm afraid it could. No one else
was shooting here. In the best of hands, Inspector, it is,
alas, possible for a rifle bullet to ricochet.'

'May I see your rifle, sir?'

Mr Henson handed him the weapon. Inspector Rogers
was a good shot himself, and he envied the balance and
finish of the rifle he now held. He looked at the magazine.
'There would appear to be four rounds gone,' he said.

'That would be right. I shoot to kill – three rabbits,
three rounds. I fired the fourth round at a rabbit near
the hedge – of course I did not know that there was anyone on the other side of the hedge. Something went
dreadfully wrong. I can only assume that the bullet must
have hit a stone and ricocheted into the hedge. I may
say that I am exceedingly careful in these matters. There
is a road beyond the hedge, and although it is not much
used there may always be some traffic on it. I would not
fire at a bird below hedge-level. A rabbit, though, is different. It is low on the ground, and a round which for
some reason doesn't hit will go harmlessly into the earth.
I miss rarely, but of course I do miss sometimes. Before I
shoot at anything I take care to see that my round can
do no harm to anything else. Unhappily, one cannot
guard against every possible accident.'

'No, sir. I wonder if we can find the stone your bullet struck?'

'Long odds against – it's rather a stony field. But obviously we must try. I'll come and hunt with you.' They began to walk towards the hedge, but were brought up by the sound of a car's stopping on the other side of it.

'That'll be the doctor, probably,' the inspector said. 'I must go and talk to him.'

Doctor and ambulance had arrived almost together, and the doctor and two ambulance men were with Jennifer and the constable as Inspector Rogers came up to them. The doctor completed his examination quickly. 'We can do nothing here – he must have been killed instantly,' he said. 'There'll have to be an autopsy, of course. The sooner we can get him away the better.'

'The information we have suggests that he may have been killed by a bullet from a .22 rifle,' the inspector said.

'From the size of the wound that seems quite probable. There's no exit wound, so the bullet must be lodged somewhere in the bony structure of the skull, and doubtless we can recover it for you.'

'That will help the forensic experts to identify the weapon from which it was fired, though at the moment there doesn't seem much doubt about this. It looks like accidental death, but of course there'll have to be an inquest.'

'Of course.' The doctor turned to the ambulance men. 'There's no point in taking him to hospital. You can go straight to the mortuary,' he said.

For Jennifer there was a miserable sense of anti-climax. She'd been keyed up for something to happen, but nothing was going to happen. 'I don't think we need keep you any more, miss,' the inspector said politely. 'You did very well to get on to us so quickly. I'm afraid you'll be called to give evidence at the inquest, but you will get notice about that. If there's anything else, we have your address and we can get in touch with you. The constable will take you back to your own car in the village.' That was that. There wasn't even lunch to look forward to, it was much too late. She'd told her father to have his usual bread and cheese, and not to wait for her to cook. As for herself, she didn't want any lunch now. And she had no heart for shopping in Oxford; in any case, there wasn't really time.

With Jennifer's departure, Mr Henson got a trifle impatient. 'You have my address, too. Do you need to keep *me* here any longer, Inspector?" he asked.

Rogers thought for a moment. 'No, sir, I don't think so,' he said. 'I have your preliminary statement. There will have to be a more formal statement for the coroner, and, of course, you will be required for the inquest. It would be helpful if you could call at headquarters later this afternoon – the superintendent will certainly wish to have a word with you. Could you manage that?'

'If you think it imperative. I have a good deal to do this afternoon. Would five o'clock be all right?'

'Yes, sir. I'll tell the superintendent. Before you go I should like to mark the place in the field where you were standing.'

'The dog brought the rabbits to my feet – it would have been precisely there.'

'I ought to mark it in your presence, sir.'

'Very well.' They walked back to the field. On the way the inspector picked up an old branch of blackthorn from the ditch, and when they got to where the rabbits were lying he asked Mr Henson to stand with the rabbits at his feet, as nearly as he could recall his position when he fired towards the hedge. The bit of blackthorn was then firmly planted where he stood. The inspector took out his notebook. 'I shall need to keep your rifle, sir. I'll write down its number and give you a receipt for it,' he said.

The magistrate handed over the weapon rather ungraciously. 'Don't you trust me with a rifle any more?' he asked.

'It's not that, sir. When the bullet is recovered we shall

need the rifle to make sure that it was one of your rounds.'

'I don't see where else it could have come from. Again I'm sorry, Inspector – I am naturally rather upset.' He called the dog to him, and they walked to the magistrate's Land Rover. 'Of course I shall do something for old Cartwright's widow,' Mr Henson said as he got in.

'I'm sure that would be proper, sir.' There are times when a policeman has to bite his tongue.

When the Land Rover had gone, Rogers went back to the road and considered the ditch. The ambulance men had left the old man's basket, with a scatter of ripe blackberries spilled beside it. They must have spilled when the old man fell, for the inspector had watched as the ambulance men carefully prised the basket from the dead hand holding it, and no berries had fallen out then. He studied the hedge itself, stood in the ditch as if he were picking blackberries, and asked the constable to go into the field and see how visible he was. 'Can't really see you at all,' the constable called back.

It was a thick hedge, particularly thick where the old man had fallen, and the inspector was prepared to accept Mr Henson's statement that he had seen no one through it. Like all old hedges, though – and this one may have gone back for six or seven centuries – it varied in texture here and there. It was thick with brambles where the old man had stood, and it was interwoven with them for most of its length to the village, though not everywhere so densely. The quality of its fruit was clearly known locally, for every few yards the grass and nettles of the ditch were trampled where blackberry pickers had gone in to reach the berries.

The blackberry is a curious fruit, capable of going from the dark purple of full ripeness to unripened red or even green in the same cluster. The degree of ripeness also varies along a hedge, berries from different roots of wild bramble ripening at different times, their ripeness also depending on the micro-climate round them, on the shade and shelter offered by the leaves of neighbouring hedge-growth. At the point where the old man had fallen the blackberry crop, although rich, seemed almost wholly red and unripe, whereas a few yards along the ditch the hedge was black with ripe fruit. There were no unripe berries in the old man's basket, nor in those spilled from it. 'Wonder why he went in there?' the inspector asked himself, adding in his mind the explanation, 'Maybe his eyes weren't all that good.'

The horrible job of breaking the news to the old man's widow had now to be faced. There could be no practical doubt of Mr Henson's identification, though there would have to be more formal evidence for the inquest – Rogers hoped that they could find some other relative to spare the widow. But she herself had to be told. Leaving the constable to search the edge of the field for a possibly bullet-chipped stone, he went alone to tell a stricken woman that her husband had been killed.

'You're not happy, George,' said the superintendent. They were in the office after the departure of Mr Henson, and the Chief Constable, who had been present at the interview with the magistrate because of the local importance of the case.

'No,' Rogers said, 'I'm not.'

'On what we've just heard the coroner will have no difficulty in recording a verdict of accidental death.'

'I know. But it was an extraordinary accident. Are you a blackberry picker?'

'Can't say I am. Go out sometimes with the family on Sundays, but that's more for a drive into the country than anything else.'

'Well, I've picked a lot of blackberries in my time, and I can't think why he was standing at a part of the hedge where there aren't any ripe ones.'

'Looking for them, I suppose.'

'No. The old boy had been an engine driver, needed

first-class eyesight for the job, and, according to his widow, kept it. Never had glasses in his life. And he'd picked at that hedge for years. It breaks your heart to think of it, but the old woman told me they'd used a retirement collection from his mates to buy a secondhand deep freeze, and for the six or seven years since he retired he'd picked enough blackberries every year to keep them going through the winter. He was a Spurbridge man, born in the cottage – his mother lived there till she died, only a few years back. He knew all about that hedge, and where the fruit is ripe and where it's not.'

'Not very convincing, George.'

'It worries me. I'm also worried about the hedge itself. The stretch where he was found is about the only place in its whole length where it really is too dense to see anything through it. If he'd been picking at almost any other place he could have been seen, not clearly, perhaps, but at least as someone moving in the hedge.'

'He wasn't seen. That's why there was an accident. Mr Henson wouldn't have fired if he'd known that anyone was there.'

'Suppose he was moved while Miss Brill went off to dial 999?'

'There's not the slightest evidence.'

'I don't know. I've been back to see Miss Brill, and as far as she can remember there weren't any blackberries spilled on the ground beside his basket when she first saw him. There were later.'

'Can she swear to that?'

'No. It can only be an impression in her mind. But it fits in with my feelings about the accident. Mr Henson was shooting at a rabbit, low on the ground. You'd expect a bullet hitting a stone at such a low angle of sight to hit the hedge a few inches from the ground. If the old man was standing on the inner bank of the ditch at the foot of the hedge, his head would have been three to four feet up, even allowing for bending.'

'A ricochet can fly off anywhere.'

'Sure. But we've found no stone with a bullet-chip on it – agreed, there are a hell of a lot of stones. And the pathologist has recovered the bullet. The rifling marks match Mr Henson's rifle, but there's no particular deformation of the bullet to suggest it hit a stone.'

'The bullet was deformed in striking the bony part of the skull – that would hide any earlier deformation from a stone.'

'Maybe. But I asked the pathologist specially about this – it was a clean wound from a high-velocity round. A deformed bullet would have made a more jagged hole in the man's forehead.'

The superintendent liked and respected Rogers. Took himself a bit too seriously sometimes, perhaps, but for all that he was a fine detective. On the other hand the evidence he had was far too slight to cast doubt on the word of a well-known local magistrate. 'Well, you've got tomorrow and the weekend,' the superintendent said. 'There won't be an inquest before Monday or Tuesday, and if you can find a scrap of positive evidence to justify an adjournment, or any verdict other than accidental death, of course the chief and I will back you. But for heaven's sake be careful, George. The man's a magistrate, and even if his story is not strictly accurate – perhaps he did move the body a bit because he felt that he ought to have seen movement in the hedge – there's not a hint of motive to give any reason for the shooting.'

Jennifer earned her half-day on Thursdays by working late on Fridays, when the dispensary stayed open late to meet the needs of patients from a late surgery that doctors at the local health centre held once a week. That Friday she did not get home at all, for she was dead.

Rogers was telephoned at home about 11 p.m. 'I know you're working on that fatality at Spurbridge, and I thought you'd like to know at once that there's been another accident on that same road by what they call

Pitt's Field. Girl driving alone in a Mini ran off the road for some reason, overturned in a ditch, and broke her neck.'

'Has she been identified?'

'From her driving licence she was a Miss Jennifer Brill, with an address at Linworth. Her father – she lived with her father – has gone to the mortuary to identify her, but I don't think there can be much doubt.'

'Right. I'll go out to Spurbridge at once. If there's a police car still there, will you ask the officers to wait till I come?'

Rogers was met by two uniformed men of the road patrol. 'What happened?' he asked.

'Don't know – and perhaps we never shall know,' the senior man replied. 'No witnesses, so we don't know even the time of the accident. There's not much on this road at night, and we were called by a motorist who simply saw the car in the ditch – might have gone in half an hour before. No other vehicle seems to have been involved. One of the front tyres of the Mini is burst, and the other damaged. Maybe in daylight we can find out how and why. There's no obvious reason to be seen at present.'

The Mini had been hauled out of the ditch by firemen called to release the woman trapped inside. Upright now, but forlornly and rather drunkenly so, it stood at the roadside. Red lights were put round it, and Rogers arranged for a police watch on the scene all night.

At first light he was back, with an expert from the road traffic department. There were skid marks on the road to show where the car had begun to slide, but nothing to suggest why. One of the front tyres had a straight slash that might almost have been done with a knife, the other a sort of burn-mark. 'Obviously hit something,' the expert said, 'but what?' He studied the wreckage of the front wheels. 'Braking's badly out of adjustment – that might explain why one tyre burst and the other didn't. Can we take away the car now for more detailed examination?' Rogers nodded. The remains of the Mini were loaded on the breakdown lorry they had brought with them.

He stayed behind. Saturday morning, and far from making any progress in investigation of the shooting there was this death added. There would be a pathologist's report later, but Rogers expected nothing from it. Preliminary medical examination of the body showed no trace or smell of alcohol, no sign of the effect of any other drug. There was nothing to be hoped for from the scientists. If the cause of the girl's death was ever to be found, it would be found here.

It would have been twilight, but need not have been quite dark when it happened. Rogers considered ways of wrecking a car. A steel cable drawn across the road? That had been used in war and various civil disturbances, and it had the advantage of being totally removable as evidence – it might also explain the slashed tyre. Such a wire would need strong supports – steel rods driven hard into the ground, for instance.

The road-marks showed where the Mini had presumably hit something and Rogers searched for possible rod-holes in the ditch. As archaeologists know, a hole in the ground is among the more indestructible works of man; even if it has been filled up, you can generally tell where it has been. The ditch showed nothing. He tried the other side of the road : no hole but something else that made his heart jump – the gnarled trunk of an ancient blackthorn with a ring of bark rubbed off it. Hard as iron and anchored by roots unshakeable in any gale, such a tree-trunk could certainly have held a cable strongly enough to wreck the Mini; and a line from the scar of the trunk crossed the road at about the right height. There *must* be something on the other side – if not in the ditch, then in the field beyond it. The hedge was too thick to get through, but it wasn't far from the gate he had used before. He went into the field and walked in-

23

side the hedge until he came to a point opposite the scar on the thorn-trunk across the road. Then he searched the ground. Yes, there was what looked like a hole made by a crowbar! No attempt had been made to fill it in. For a moment this shook his thinking, and then he realised that there would have been no need. Fields have all sorts of holes in them, and whoever made this hole would not expect anyone to come looking for it. Besides, it would have been almost dark, and – he shivered slightly – there might have been urgent work to be done in the ditch. Now the pathologists would have more to consider than the time of last meal and the possibilities of drink. They would have to find out whether the broken neck could have been assisted manually.

Rogers felt that he could see the events of last night as if they were being played out on a stage. The site was well chosen: the ground rose from the hedge, and a watcher by the crowbar-hole could see over the top. The prepared trip wire, anchored to the blackthorn, would lie harmlessly across the road should any other car come by. The Mini seen, a quick pull and a couple of turns round the crowbar would make the wire lethal. . . . Then he pulled himself together. The hole and the marks on the tree-trunk were real evidence, but it was evidence that could be explained away, and the rest was pure speculation. And why? He'd got to find more facts. Another thought flashed into the forefront of the jumble in his mind – a seemingly irrelevant thought. Why was it called Pitt's Field?

The inspector was a Wessex man and he knew that it was common enough for big fields to have names, often marked – as this one was – on Ordnance maps. But in this district 'Field' was a rarity; a field would more usually be called, after some long-gone owner or tenant, So-and-So's 'Piece'. He said to himself aloud, 'I wonder . . . just possible, I suppose. . . .'

He called the superintendent from the radio-telephone in his car, asked for urgent instructions to be given to the pathologists, and said that he would call again later with, he hoped, important information. The superintendent was impressed but still cautious. 'Don't forget the man's a magistrate,' he said.

Rogers drove back into Spurbridge and called at the Vicarage. Yes, there were still some parish registers in the church, and they could be inspected for a small fee – 'It doesn't go to me, but to the diocese,' the vicar added. He took Rogers to the vestry of the village church, where the registers lived in an ancient iron safe. 'Have they ever been indexed?' the inspector asked.

'As a matter of fact they have,' the vicar replied unexpectedly. 'We have a quite well-known local historian in the village, and she indexed them for us a few years back.'

'Then I think all I need is to have a look at the index.'

The vicar, a little puzzled, handed him a folder with a batch of typed sheets. Rogers glanced at it and gave it back. 'Thanks very much indeed,' he said. 'How much is the fee?'

'But you've not even looked at the registers . . . I can't take any fee.'

'Please . . . as a contribution to the church.'

The vicar remained puzzled, but Rogers went away content. 'It's not conclusive, of course, but it may mean something,' he said to himself. 'At least there's no record of any family called Pitt.'

He went back to headquarters and had a long talk with the superintendent, who called in the Chief Constable. Although it was Saturday morning the chief came in at once. While they were talking the telephone rang in the superintendent's office. He took the call, and when he had put down the phone he said, 'That was the pathologist with a preliminary report. The girl was wearing a seat belt, and although he cannot say conclusively, the injury to her neck is more consistent with some form of manual garotting than with striking anything in the car. She had other injuries in the crash which might have caused unconsciousness, but were not sufficient to cause death. He has other tests to make before he can give us a full report, but he felt that we should know of his preliminary finding as soon as possible.'

'Quite right,' the Chief Constable said. He considered things for a few moments, and summed up judicially. 'There is still a lot of speculation in Inspector Rogers's :deas, but the pathologist's findings go some way towards justifying at least some of them,' he said. 'There is a case to answer, but for the moment I don't think we can go farther than that. We need more hard evidence before making an arrest – an untimely arrest might do great harm. You must continue inquiries urgently, and keep me directly informed.'

Rogers and the superintendent arranged a plan of action. It was a simple plan. It required a call by the superintendent at Spurbridge Manor that afternoon, to keep Mr Henson occupied while the inspector went blackberrying.

Inspector Rogers equipped himself with a basket for the benefit of possible passers-by, but his expedition included another police vehicle with four officers and equipment not normally needed for blackberrying. The police van waited in a side road, and Rogers parked his car on the verge by the blackberry hedge. He went into the ditch at the patch of berries – most of them still red and unripe – by which the old railwayman had been found.

In the inspector's view the death of Jennifer Brill so soon after that of the old man could mean only one thing – that there was something of desperate importance to a murderer to be found in the ditch, and that whatever it was it would not be discovered where the old man had been found. That meant, as he had suspected all along, that the body had been moved, and that in turn implied that Jennifer had been killed because she was the only person who might be able to say if the body had been moved. The stick marking the place from which Mr Henson had been shooting was clearly visible in the field. To the right of the unripe blackberries the rise of ground in the field soon masked the view of the stick from the hedge – and of the hedge from the stick. So Rogers decided to work away to the left.

It was not possible to tell from the condition of grass and nettles in the ditch where a body might have fallen, for there was considerable trampling from other blackberry pickers. He made his way steadily along the ditch picking blackberries as he went, partly to dispel suspicion – though there seemed nobody else about on the quiet road – partly because by repeating the old railwayman's actions he might stand a better chance of learning what, if anything, he might have come upon. A dozen or so yards from the patch of red berries was a section of hedge bearing a mass of luscious ripe ones. These ripe berries were borne on rather long strands of bramble which remained unmatted, making the hedge itself less dense. Rogers could see through the hedge to the stick, and he had no doubt that anyone standing by the stick could have seen him, or at least made out his movements. A white forehead, for instance, could certainly have been seen. But why, why, why . . .? There was nothing here but ditch and blackberry hedge. The idea of murder was ridiculous. The girl's death was simply one of those coincidences that do happen in life, and the pathologist must just be wrong about the cause of injury to her neck. . . .

Then his left leg sank into the ground. His right foot remained firm, and he saved himself from going down by clutching at the hedge, getting severely scratched in doing so. A moment later he forgot all about scratched hands. As he regained his balance and looked into the hole he saw it was the mouth of a sort of tunnel running under the hedge. . . .

He went to his own car and called up the van. When

27.

it came the police erected temporary screens to hide what they were doing from the road. One uniformed man stood in the road to deal with any possible traffic, three men took off their jackets and got down into the ditch with spades. After digging for a few minutes round the hole in the ditch, Rogers sent two of the men into the field, to start digging on the other side of the hedge.

'God, I'm digging into a pile of bones,' one of the men called out.

'They'll be mostly old bones, at least three hundred years old,' Rogers said. 'But we must get them out to see if there are any newer ones among them.'

There were, but these newer bones were still attached to flesh – the pathetic remains of a little girl, in a polka-dot red and white dress. The dress answered a description they all knew. 'Julie Summers!' two of them said together.

That was the name of the twelve-year-old schoolgirl who had disappeared on her way home from school in a London suburb about a month ago. The papers and news bulletins had been full of it. Another small girl said she thought she had seen Julie getting into a car, but that was as far as anyone could get and inevitably new sensations displaced the Julie Summers story in the news. Now the police had found her . . . and more digging brought to light the remains of two more little female bodies. Julie, and the other little girls, had all had their necks broken, and all appeared to have been sexually outraged. That was certain in Julie's case, but one of the others had been buried for two years, the other for three, and although the cause of death seemed certain the rest had to be to some extent conjecture.

Not much conjecture, though. Mr Henson had begun by denying everything, but a search of Spurbridge Manor revealed a disgusting range of pornographic and sado-pornographic material, and the more the police investigated, the more they found. The easiest of the multiple murders to prove turned out to be that of Jennifer Brill, for a length of steel wire with traces of blackthorn-bark and of rubber from the Mini's tyres still adhering to it, was found in a barn at the Manor. Substantial evidence of the abduction of little Julie came to light when a wisp of her long fair hair was found in Mr Henson's car. He was charged with five murders, but the Crown decided to proceed initially with two – those of Jennifer and Julie. At first Mr Henson entered pleas of Not Guilty, but after prosecuting counsel's opening statement he changed his plea to Guilty, and all his own counsel could do for him was to plead that he was sick. 'Sick you may indeed be,' the judge sai l, 'but it is a sickness too dangerous for society to tolerate. A man capable of acting as a magistrate and judging others can scarcely ask anyone to believe that he is incapable of responsibility for his own actions.' Henson was given concurrent sentences of life imprisonment, the judge adding that in his view the sentence of life imprisonment in this case should mean imprisonment for life.

When it was all over the judge sent for Inspector Rogers, who was taken into the Judge's Room by the Chief Constable. 'With the plea of Guilty,' the judge said, 'police evidence was not called, and although of course I have the papers I am still puzzled – and greatly interested – by what seems to me an outstanding piece of detection.'

'That is just what it was,' the Chief Constable said.

'It is generous of you to say so, sir, but really it was more a matter of history,' said Inspector (though he was now Chief Inspector) Rogers. 'Partly it was my own childhood history of blackberrying – I *knew* that no experienced blackberry picker would waste time in scrambling through a ditch to get at a hedge of red berries. Miss Brill's murder made it obvious that there was some compelling reason for shooting the old man – and again it was history that led us to what it was. I've always been interested in local names and I wondered why it was

Pitt's *Field* instead of Pitt's *Piece*. Suddenly it occurred to me that it might have nothing to do with anyone called Pitt, but might derive from a seventeenth-century plague pit, which might have given its name to a "Field" because no one wanted to own it as a "Piece". Several of these villages were badly affected by the plague of 1665 and by earlier plagues going back to medieval times, brought by refugees from London. When there were a lot of deaths from plague there was no time – and perhaps little inclination – for normal grave-digging, and there would be mass burials in pits. Since people were afraid of handling any more than they had to those who died from plague, it was reasonable to suppose that they would have used a pit that could be reached straight from the roadside. Henson, who was a genuine farmer and who often drove his own tractors must have discovered the old pit – and found it useful for his other activities. The wet summer followed an exceptionally dry one, and where the entrance to the old plague-pit had been filled in the ground had weathered away. Henson must have seen the old man poking about precisely where he knew it was most dangerous to him, and shot him forthwith. I doubt if the old man thought anything of the hole except as a place to keep out of, but the danger was in Henson's mind. The rest followed. Given more time he would doubtless have filled in the hole again. He didn't have time.'

'Thanks to your detective work – or should I say sense of history?'

'I think, my Lord, they come to much the same thing.'

N. J. Crisp

MURDER IS EASY

It began with a 999 call.

'Emergency. Which service do you require?'

'Police.'

Detective Inspector Sidney Kenyon was opening a bottle of wine in his basement flat in Gloucester Terrace, W.2, when the phone started to ring. The drawn curtains hid the light snow which was falling on his patio outside, and the glowing electric fire had boosted the panel heating considerably, turning the living room into a warm, cosy, comfortable place.

Kenyon glanced at his watch. 'Sod it,' he said. 'I thought I'd got away with it.'

'Could be a wrong number,' Ann suggested. Her fair hair glinted as she turned her head, and smiled at him.

'Don't bet your dowry on it,' Kenyon said sourly. He lifted the receiver. 'Kenyon.'

'Sorry, Sid,' Detective Sergeant Len Mallory said.

'You will be, mate,' Kenyon said, 'if this could have waited until tomorrow.' He listened to the even voice of his detective sergeant, who was speaking from Bayswater Police Station, and reluctantly made some notes. 'Okay,' he said. 'See you there.' He hung up and looked at Ann. 'Some silly bugger's got himself murdered,' he said. He picked up his keys, his briefcase, and pulled on his raincoat.

'Oh,' Ann said. She sat up straight, and arranged her

skirt nervously over her slim legs. She was still not entirely used to the exigencies of a copper's life.

'You go to bed,' Kenyon said. 'I'll be back later.'

'How long will you be?'

'No longer than I can bloody help,' Kenyon said.

Outside, the night air, although still, cut like a jagged knife. A fragile layer of snow was frozen to the windscreen of Kenyon's car. He shivered, bad-temperedly scraped it off, and drove to the address Mallory had given him, a block of flats in Halden Road, near Ladbroke Grove.

Among the vehicles parked outside was the patrol car which had answered the 999 call, placed by a Mrs Mason.

'She noticed the door of his flat was open, sir,' the driver told Kenyon. 'The lights were on inside. She called, got no answer. She said they get prowlers, seeing if there's anything they can knock off. She was afraid to go in, so she dialled 999.'

'So who found the body?' Kenyon enquired. 'You?' The driver nodded. 'And who decided it was murder, which gets me called out?' Kenyon asked, coldly. 'Instead of an accident, which wouldn't?'

'I didn't think he'd bashed his own head in, sir,' the driver said.

Kenyon grunted, forbore to point out the damage that could be inflicted by a fall, went inside along the corridor to the ground floor flat, and found Mallory. Kenyon guessed the excited, birdlike woman he was talking to was Mrs Mason. He caught Mallory's eye, acknowledged the half wink, skirted the pair of them, and made his way along the narrow hall to where the activity was.

'Evening, sir,' Kenyon said.

'Hullo, Sid,' the police surgeon said.

Kenyon looked round the bedroom, ignoring the photographer, who ignored him as he carefully took his endless shots of the subject, who was lying on the floor, wearing shirt and slacks, and had no need to worry about holding his pose.

Fingerprints were already at work, dusting meticulously. Kenyon nodded to the two men from Forensic who wandered in. They appeared to be looking forward to a long night about as much as Kenyon was.

'Hand on heart, I can certify that this man is dead,' the police surgeon said, which was all he was required to do at this stage of the proceedings.

'With half his brains all over the carpet,' Kenyon said, 'I'm not surprised. Come on, doctor. Take a chance.'

'Probably the traditional blunt instrument,' the police surgeon said, cautiously, 'from the way his skull's been stove in. More than one blow, in all likelihood.'

'Could be,' Kenyon agreed. But there was no sign of any blunt instrument, which could have hair and blood adhering to it. Kenyon gave some instructions, went to the living room, lit a cigarette, and waited for Mallory.

The furniture was from Habitat. The room was illuminated by adjustable variable intensity spotlights. There was a video cassette recorder, as well as a television set. The occupant liked books and music. Or had done so, before his life came to an abrupt end.

Kenyon stubbed out his cigarette and lit another one. He wished he had had enough common sense to shove half a bottle of whisky into his raincoat pocket. Even that wine, which he had opened for Ann's benefit, would be welcome.

Mallory strolled in, writing neatly in his notebook on the move.

'There's a pub down the road,' Kenyon said. 'Let's go and have a drink.'

Outside, a team of policemen had started to comb the area, searching gardens, gutters, drains, dustbins, any place where the murderer might have hurriedly disposed of the object with which Roger Sanders had been killed. In Kenyon's experience a panic-stricken man or woman would be anxious to get rid of such an incriminating object. Assuming he or she *was* panic-stricken.

Kenyon bought two large scotches, swigged half of his in one go, and felt the warmth he needed seeping into his veins. Mallory turned the pages of his notebook back. He was a good Detective Sergeant, skilled in putting together an outline picture fast.

'Roger Sanders,' Mallory said. 'Age thirty-one. Occupation commercial artist, worked for an advertising agency.'

'Did you get any gossip from Mrs Mason?' Kenyon interrupted.

'No.' Mallory said. 'Just times, and so on. He came home from work just after six o'clock. She'd been shopping, met him on the way in. He said, "Brass-monkey weather this", which she thought was rather crude. At nine o'clock, she was taking her rubbish down. That's when she noticed that his door was open.'

'Any known callers between six and nine?'

'Not so far,' Mallory said, 'and I don't fancy our chances, with him being on the ground floor near the back entrance. Most of the other residents use the lift.'

'Only one suspect so far then,' Kenyon remarked. 'Mrs Mason.'

Mallory grinned. 'I reckon she's a potential victim, one of these fine days,' he said. 'She'd drive me potty in no time flat. God knows how her husband puts up with her.'

'Your turn,' Kenyon said, pushing his empty glass across the table.

Mallory fetched refills. When he came back, his expression was thoughtful. 'Roger Sanders was single,' he said. 'There's some pretty fancy gear in his wardrobe. Maybe he's a pooffter. The jealousy bit. They sometimes get carried away.'

'There's a jar of moisturising cream on his dressing table,' Kenyon said.

'That could be his,' Mallory argued.

34

'Well, Fingerprints'll tell us,' Kenyon said. 'But he's also got cassettes of blue movies in his living room, and they're not the homo kind.'

Momentary irritation flitted across Mallory's amiable features. His eye for detail was not yet as good as Kenyon's and it sometimes annoyed him.

'I've got nothing else to do but hang around while you're doing the work,' Kenyon said, kindly. 'One more, and then we'll go back.' He thought of phoning Ann, who would probably be playing Peggy Lee records, but decided against it. The sooner he got this wrapped up, the sooner he could get home again.

Kenyon interviewed Mrs Mason in her flat on the second floor, which was clinically, if not pathologically, clean and tidy. Mallory was searching the dead man's flat with meticulous care, and could safely be left to get on with it. Other officers were interviewing the remaining residents of the block, which should have had a porter, but did not, the previous incumbent having proved difficult to replace. Kenyon thought that was a nuisance. Porters were useful fellows. Usually, what they knew about residents would alarm the latter considerably. But Mrs Mason proved to be a good substitute.

'Some girl used to live with him,' she said, disapprovingly. 'Not that I pry into other people's business, of course . . .'

'Of course not,' Kenyon said.

'But they made no secret of it,' Mrs Mason said. 'Mail used to come for her at his address.'

'So you might possibly recall her name,' Kenyon said.

'Sally Fry,' Mrs Mason said, promptly. 'They were together, oh, it must have been nearly two years.'

'Do you happen to know why they might have split up?' Kenyon enquired.

'I rather gather that he'd thrown her out, that would be before Christmas, and she was being difficult about it, making scenes, ringing him up in the middle of the night,

35

and so on.' Mrs Mason contemplated her wedding ring, and seemed to think she should account for her possession of this intimate knowledge. 'I wouldn't dream of listening to any gossip, of course, but Mr Sanders sometimes seemed to feel the need to confide in me, for some reason.'

'Of course,' Kenyon said. He thought that was one of the more unlikely yarns he had heard that week. 'Did Miss Fry ever come back to the flat to your knowledge?'

'Only on New Year's Eve, as far as I know,' Mrs Mason said. 'There was a whole crowd of them . . . his friends, I suppose . . . Miss Fry was one of them, somewhat drunk. My husband and I happened to be returning from a function when they all arrived.'

'Yes,' Kenyon said. 'Has Mr Sanders had any other lady visitors that you're aware of?'

'Only the dark girl, who . . .' Mrs Mason began. She stopped, and looked at Kenyon curiously. 'Why are you so interested in lady friends, Inspector? No woman could possibly have done such an awful savage thing.'

The nosy old bag must have taken a look into the bedroom, Kenyon thought. 'As a matter of fact, that's not quite true, Mrs Mason,' he said. 'But apart from that, I do have my reasons. This dark girl, who was she?'

'I don't know,' Mrs Mason said. 'I happened to notice her leaving on, I think, three mornings. He must have ordered a taxi for her. I'm afraid Mr Sanders led a somewhat irregular life, by normal standards.'

'I'm sure,' Kenyon said. 'Could you describe this girl?'

'Tall, very slim, long black hair. I suppose some people might have found her attractive,' Mrs Mason said, reluctantly. 'Late twenties, perhaps.'

The corpse had been removed for its post mortem. Forensic were still painstakingly combing everything, and would no doubt eventually come up with a human hair, or a tiny fragment of fibre which did not belong in the flat, in due course. Kenyon had no intention of waiting. He regarded post mortems, Forensic and Fingerprints as props. They might supply evidence which would knit together at a trial, but it was his business to solve murders, not theirs.

Mallory was busy checking the dead man's personal effects, and the kind of documents men accumulate. He indicated pay slips and bank statements.

'Bloody well paid,' Mallory said, 'but nothing in the bank.'

'Sally Fry,' Kenyon said.

'I know about her,' Mallory said. 'Letters and things. The original idea was that they'd get married, one day. The flat was half hers. That's where his money's gone, trying to pay her off. She got very uptight when he chucked her out. Some of these letters are vitriolic . . . enough to make your hair curl.'

'Fine,' Kenyon said, happily. 'So let's find out where the lady was between six and nine this evening.'

'At home with her parents, who live in Newbury,' Mallory said, smugly. 'I checked ten minutes ago.'

'Oh,' Kenyon said. He supposed that Mallory had evened the score. He fidgeted with his cigarette lighter, depressed. It all made such good sense. A woman scorned . . . the odds were she still had her keys to the flat . . . another quarrel . . . striking Sanders from behind with some heavy object . . . striking him again and again in a frenzy as he fell to the floor . . . a good suspect with the right emotional involvement.

Instead of which, she was at home with her bloody parents, miles away, Kenyon thought, disgusted. He reluctantly abandoned Sally Fry.

'According to Mrs Mason,' Kenyon said, 'Roger's been screwing some tall, slim bird, with long dark hair, since he chucked Sally out. Name not known. See what's in his little black book.'

Mallory went through the dead man's pocket diary. 'Well, let's see,' he said. 'Early in January, "Dinner with J. Will phone her next week".' He turned a page. 'Here we are. "J. stayed. An easy fuck. Does everything".'

'Charming,' Kenyon said.

Mallory turned some more pages. 'He kept score,' he said. 'The lady obliged twice more, at weekly intervals, with appropriate comments on her eager willingness.'

'Mrs Mason doesn't miss a trick,' Kenyon said.

'There's also some girl called A.,' Mallory said, 'whom he took to lunch, and had drinks with a couple of times recently.'

'Did that suffice to get her to bed as well?' Kenyon enquired.

'Apparently she's a bit more difficult,' Mallory said. 'Or more choosy.'

'These ladies must have names as well as initials,' Kenyon said. 'And preferably addresses.'

Mallory turned to the back of the diary, and shook his head. 'Jane just has a phone number,' he said. 'So has Angela.'

'Very occasionally,' Kenyon said, 'even our primitive telephone system can be induced to work.'

Mallory went into the hall and tested this proposition. Kenyon listened to the soft murmur of his voice, yawned, lit a cigarette, and smoked it until he came back.

'Angela is a model,' Mallory said, 'and not at home. She's working in Paris.'

'The man's women certainly bloody travel,' Kenyon complained. 'Where's Jane? Heading up the Nile?'

'In a top-floor flat off Queensway,' Mallory said. 'She shares with two other girls. Her name's Miss Jane Parker.'

'Thank God for that,' Kenyon said. He stood up. 'I was beginning to think we'd have to arrest Mrs Mason.'

They rode to the top floor of the ageing block in an antiquated lift, and rang the doorbell. A plump girl opened the door, let them in, and introduced herself as Kate.

Jane Parker was drinking coffee in the kitchen. Mallory had not explained why they wanted to see her, and her attitude was curious, but not apprehensive. Kenyon thought that if she knew anything about Roger Sanders' death, she was a damn good actress.

Well, that could be, but she was not what the diary entries might lead anyone to expect. Her voice was musical and low pitched, her manner modest, and almost shy. Kenyon asked if they could speak in private, and she led them along the corridor to her room. It was well-furnished, with a single bed, armchairs, and a stereo record player. Mallory closed the door.

'Well, please sit down,' Jane said. 'I don't know what this is all about.'

'Are you acquainted with a man called Roger Sanders?' Kenyon asked.

Jane blinked. 'I know him,' she said cautiously. 'Why?'

Kenyon ignored the query. 'How well do you know him?'

'We're friends,' Jane said.

'Would I be correct in saying,' Kenyon said, 'that your friendship extends to sleeping with him?'

Jane's cheeks coloured. 'If you're really from the police,' she said sharply, 'I'd like to see your warrant card.'

Kenyon eyed her curiously. 'Why should you doubt that we're policemen?' he asked.

'Your warrant card, please,' Jane said.

Kenyon showed it to her. She examined it carefully, and slowly gave it back to him.

'Who did you think we were?' Kenyon enquired.

'I don't know . . . the questions you were asking . . .'

'Private detectives?'

'I don't understand this at all,' Jane said.

'Who do you think might employ private detectives to interview you, Miss Parker?'

'I want to know why you should ask me about Roger Sanders,' Jane said.

'Because he's dead,' Kenyon said.

'Dead?'

Kenyon said nothing. He watched her face and hands

closely, noting every tiny change of expression, every nervous movement. Somewhere a telephone had started to ring.

Jane shook her head helplessly like a woman who was shocked. But there were no signs of tears in her eyes. 'When? What happened?' Her voice had ascended a few notes. 'An accident?'

'He was murdered,' Kenyon said.

'Oh, my God,' Jane said. She sat down abruptly on the bed. Her face lost its colour. Her right hand flew involuntarily to her mouth.

There was a tap on the door, and Kate opened it. 'Sorry to interrupt,' she said, 'but there's a phone call for you, Jane. It's Colin.' Her eyes were inquisitive as she stared at the shaken Jane.

'Oh . . . yes . . .' Jane pushed her hair back as though confronted by some insoluble problem.

'I told him you had people here,' Kate said, 'but he said you'd left a message for him to call.'

'Yes,' Jane said vaguely. 'I phoned him before I went out . . .'

'Shall I say you'll ring back?' Kate asked.

'Detective Sergeant Mallory will tell you what to say,' Kenyon said.

Mallory went out with Kate. Kenyon offered Jane a cigarette. She took it gratefully, and he lit it for her.

'Where did you go this evening?' Kenyon asked, casually.

'A pottery class,' Jane said. 'I go every week.'

'What time did it finish tonight?'

'About eight-thirty, I think,' Jane said, dully.

'What did you do then?'

'Oh . . . several of us went to a Wimpy Bar and had hamburgers . . .' Jane gestured vaguely '. . . then I came home.'

Kenyon sighed. If that checked out, Jane Parker could be eliminated from his enquiries. If he went on like this, he would eliminate everybody, and end up with nobody.

'Who's Colin?' he tried.

'Colin? . . . oh . . . he's my husband,' Jane said.

One of the first things Kenyon had automatically noted was that Jane was not wearing any rings. 'I didn't realise you were married,' he said. 'You call yourself Miss.'

'We've been separated for nearly a year,' Jane said.

'But you and your husband keep in touch.'

'We used to meet occasionally,' Jane said, 'talking about divorce . . . and things like that, but eventually . . . oh, anyway, that doesn't matter . . .'

'Tell me,' Kenyon said. 'I'm interested.'

'We lived in Bristol,' Jane said. 'Colin's an accountant. He's quite a lot older than I am. I was a copywriter with a small agency there. Then I was offered a job with a top agency in London. Not much money, but a chance . . . the sort of opportunity I'd always dreamed off. Colin could have worked in London, but he wouldn't move. His mother's old . . . she likes to see him all the time . . . I felt I was in an awful, boring rut . . . perhaps I did the wrong thing, but I left, and took the job in London.'

'Is that how you met Roger Sanders?'

Jane nodded. 'The last week or so, Colin's been staying at a hotel in London. We've been seeing each other. He's a very kind man . . . affectionate . . . he still wants me . . . and now he's hoping to line up a job with a firm of accountants in the West End.'

'So you decided to get together again,' Kenyon supposed.

'Not exactly,' Jane said. 'Not that definite. But to see more of each other, with no commitment, and perhaps see if we could work something out . . . or not. But at least to try, as best we could.'

'In that case,' Kenyon wondered, 'how did Roger Sanders come into the picture?'

'That was before Colin and I decided,' Jane said. 'I'd met Roger, he was a nice chap, I liked him.'

'But no more,' Kenyon said.

'I hadn't been with anyone since I left Colin,' Jane said, 'and I suppose I felt like a bit of the other. Oh, at first, perhaps I hoped something might come of it, but I soon realised he was just using me.'

'In what way?' Kenyon asked.

'In bed,' Jane said. 'It was all very athletic, yes, but there was no love, no affection, and I don't really want to be thrown round the bed all the time. Then Roger suggested we watch blue movies, and smoke pot, and I told him I wasn't interested. Anyway, it turned out he was crazy about a model called Angela. That was why he'd chucked his previous girl-friend out. Angela's living with an actor, and won't leave him. She doesn't mind having secret lunches with Roger . . . or didn't, I keep forgetting he's dead . . . but she wouldn't sleep with him. I suppose he was getting frustrated.' She shrugged. 'He was feeling randy, and so was I, and that's it.'

'A complex series of relationships,' Kenyon said, neutrally.

'It's all crap anyway,' Jane said. 'I should have stuck to Colin.' She stared at Kenyon. She was more together now, probably as the result of talking about herself. 'Who'd want to kill Roger?'

'That's what I'm trying to establish,' Kenyon said. 'I don't think I need trouble you any more tonight.'

'I only wish I could have been of some help,' Jane said.

'You have,' Kenyon said. 'May I ask if you're always so straightforward?'

'If I think something, I say it,' Jane said. 'That's the way I am.'

'Well, I'll say good night,' Kenyon said. He turned for the door, and paused like a man about to come out with some meaningless courtesy. 'Oh, I hope things work out between you and your husband.'

'Thank you,' Jane said.

Kenyon gave her the warm, kindly, friendly smile he was good at wearing. 'I suppose you told him about Roger Sanders.'

'He asked me if there'd been anyone,' Jane said. 'There was no point in lying. I told him what had happened.'

'How did he take it?' Kenyon asked, the interested friend.

'There was a row,' Jane said. 'But as I pointed out, I wasn't with him at the time. Anyway, it wasn't important. In a way, it was because of that we might get together again.'

Kenyon nodded. 'Good night,' he said. 'If I need to speak to you again, I'll be in touch.'

'Just a minute,' Jane said. She stood up abruptly. It was apparent that something had clicked inside her head. She stared at him with startled, wide eyes. He could almost trace her dawning, horrified realisation that not one of his questions had been idle, that each had a defined purpose. And what that purpose was. 'Inspector,' Jane breathed, '. . . please . . . he couldn't . . .'

'Go to bed,' Kenyon said. 'And don't bother to make any phone calls. There's nothing you can do.'

He closed the door of her room behind him, and walked along the corridor towards the waiting Mallory. Poor mixed-up bitch, he thought.

From there on, it was all downhill.

Kenyon and Mallory drove to the hotel in Devonshire Terrace, and talked to the receptionist, the hall porter, and the housekeeper. Kenyon told Mallory what to do, and went back to Halden Road. The search seemed to be over. The team of men had gone. A uniformed sergeant was waiting.

'We found this, sir,' he said. 'It was in a dustbin belonging to a block called Hillgate Court. Round the corner. About a hundred yards away.'

Kenyon took the object, which was heavy, and wrapped in newspaper. Carefully, he peeled back the crumpled grubby paper. Inside, was an ornate, ornamental brass candlestick. Most of it picked up and reflected the

43

street lights. The base did not. There, dark, ugly irregular stains reflected nothing.

'Thanks,' Kenyon said. He re-arranged the newspaper over the candlestick, slipped it into a plastic bag, went inside, and walked along to the dead man's flat. A constable posted at the door let him in. The flat was quiet and empty. The constable was the only one left. Kenyon sat down, and lit a cigarette. There were only three left in the packet, but he thought that would be enough. There was a full packet in his office at Bayswater Police Station and he expected to be there before very long.

Ten minutes later, Mallory walked in with Colin Parker.

Kenyon guessed that Parker was in his late forties. He wore a neat light grey suit, brown shoes, an overcoat, and suede gloves. He was tall and well built, although he walked with a slight stoop. His face was pale and worried, but when he essayed a not altogether successful smile of greeting, Kenyon could see why Jane had described him as a kind man. His face changed then, and showed inner reserves of warmth and affection. Kenyon was not surprised. They came in all shapes and sizes. Every human being had the potential for it, in Kenyon's belief.

Kenyon wasted no time. 'I believe you knew of your wife's association with the dead man, Roger Sanders?' he said.

'She told me,' Parker muttered.

'Did you meet Sanders for the first time tonight?' Kenyon asked.

'I've never met him,' Parker said. 'I don't even know what he looks like.'

Kenyon had some sympathy for him. Parker spent his life dealing with balance sheets, profit and loss accounts, talking to clients and Inspectors of Taxes, a conventional man in a respected occupation. A man who cared for his ageing mother, who was devoted to his wayward wife, whose way of life called for him to abide faithfully by every rule and regulation.

44

The idea of being tried for murder, of serving a life sentence in an overcrowded prison among hardened criminals, must be an inconceivable nightmare to such a man. But it was a nightmare he had brought upon himself, and the sooner he accepted it the better. Kenyon wanted to get home.

'I think you do know him, Mr Parker,' Kenyon said. 'I think you came to this flat this evening.' Parker was shaking his head. Kenyon ignored him, and went on talking. He took the candlestick from the plastic bag and unwrapped it. 'We have reason to believe this could have been the murder weapon,' Kenyon said. 'Possibly, it stood upon the dining table over there. Examination will show whether it has the killer's fingerprints on it or not.' He stared at Parker's gloved hands. 'The murderer might, of course, have been wearing gloves, but other evidence will be available to us in due course.' He stared deep into Parker's eyes. 'According to the hotel staff, you were wearing a dark blue suit when you went out earlier this evening. When you got back, you gave it to the housekeeper for cleaning. Why did you do that, Mr Parker?'

'It needed cleaning, that's all,' Parker said. 'I have an important interview soon, and . . .'

'That suit will be removed for Forensic examination before it's cleaned,' Kenyon said. 'Which will not disturb you, if you have nothing to fear.'

Parker seemed to have a great deal to fear. His face was grey, and beads of perspiration had appeared on his temples.

'We may find bloodstains from the dead man,' Kenyon said, conversationally. 'Or perhaps microscopic fibres, if you knelt on a carpet. If so we can prove which carpet. Even particles of dust adhering to the welts of the black shoes you were wearing before. You see, Mr Parker,' Kenyon told him, 'it's only fair to warn you that by these methods, Forensic can prove beyond any shadow of doubt whether you have been here earlier this evening or not.'

This was not strictly true. Forensic could sometimes

perform miracles. Equally often, they failed to provide evidence for something which Kenyon knew had happened. But Parker was not to know that. Kenyon waited. From the corner of his eye, he caught sight of Mallory sneaking a look at his watch, and smothering a yawn.

The silence in the room grew and enveloped the three men until it was absolute and oppressive. Kenyon held the candlestick in its plastic bag, and stared at Parker. He was going. Kenyon could feel it. Any minute now . . .

Parker began to cry silently. His body shook. He covered his eyes with his gloved hands. Kenyon relaxed and lit his last cigarette. He knew that Parker would talk now. He would have to talk.

Mallory took out his notebook. Kenyon murmured the obligatory caution, but it was doubtful if Parker heard him.

'I . . . I came to tell him to leave Jane alone . . .' Parker gasped. '. . . that's all . . . I swear that was all . . . but when I saw him . . . he was so casual . . . he kept smiling . . . I knew he was laughing at me . . . I saw the cassettes . . . Jane had told me about the blue movies . . . she'd told me everything . . . he was going out . . . he went into the bedroom to put a tie on . . . something came over me . . . that bed . . . I could see them together . . . doing it . . . and he was shrugging his shoulders, and saying, "No one made her, you know. She was only too willing" . . . I don't remember what happened then . . . I honestly don't remember . . . I found myself holding the candlestick, and he was crumpled up on the floor . . . there was blood on my sleeve . . . if only I hadn't come . . . it was seeing him . . . thinking about them together . . .'

'Your wife didn't really care about him,' Kenyon said. 'She cares about you.'

'She went with him,' Parker said.

It was six o'clock in the morning when Kenyon let himself into his flat. He made tea, drank a cup, decided against a second, went to the bathroom, scrubbed his teeth, undressed, and slipped into bed.

Ann had put a pair of his pyjamas on. Kenyon started to take them off. She stirred and murmured sleepily. 'What time is it?'

'The middle of the night,' Kenyon said, caressing her body.

'Did you find out who did it?'

'Nine times out of ten,' Kenyon said, 'murder's easy. Much simpler than robbery or rape. It's nearly always family or lovers. Usually jealousy or hatred or both. You talk to a few people,' he said, stroking her, 'and you find the right one. It's not hard.'

After that, they stopped talking for a while.

Later Ann got up to go to the bathroom. When she came back, she snapped the light on, and started dressing hurriedly.

'You bastard,' she said. 'You told me it was the middle of the night. It's nearly eight o'clock. You know I've got to go home and change and get to work.'

'You'll make it,' Kenyon said, drowsily. 'I'll call you next week. Perhaps fix something for my day off.'

Ann's movements slowed down. 'Sid,' she said, 'I don't know about next week. I meant to talk to you last night, but you were called out . . .'

'Talk to me about what?' Kenyon asked, more out of politeness than curiosity.

'I've been seeing Frank,' Ann said.

Kenyon's eyes snapped wide open. 'I thought you were supposed to be getting bloody divorced,' he said.

'Well, we might not,' Ann said.

Kenyon studied her speculatively as she adjusted her tights. 'Just out of interest,' he said, 'how much does Frank know about me?'

'Not a lot,' Ann said.

'That might be the best thing,' Kenyon said. 'I met a very honest lady last night. She spoke the plain un-varnished truth. Probably to hurt someone, but that's by the way. One man died, and another'll serve ten years inside as a result.'

'God, I'm going to be late,' Ann said. 'Must go.' She kissed him quickly, and went.

Kenyon wondered whether to set the alarm and try and get an hour's sleep, but it hardly seemed worth it. He was due at the Magistrates' Court at ten o'clock.

He supposed Ann knew what she was doing, but it was a pity in a way. He liked Ann . . .

David Fletcher

MASS MURDER

Requiem aeternam

The room looks nice. I'm glad I cleaned it thoroughly
before I went out. The record player on, not too loud.
Not to disturb the neighbours. Not at this hour. It's
amazing how calm I am. Ah, the tea. The cup that
refreshes but does not inebriate, as Mother always used to
say. My hand shakes. Perhaps I am not quite so calm as
I thought. But why should I not be? Eternal rest, O Lord.
I'm not so sure about the eternal light. To purify them,
I suppose. Well, they'll certainly need that! It's done. I
can hardly believe it. A vow paid to thee in Jerusalem.
Well not quite, not exactly Jerusalem, but then *I* didn't
choose the setting. They did. Giggling and plotting it.
The look on their faces when they saw me! Mind you,
anyone would look, well, surprised in *those* circumstances.
Really I feel quite elated. How white his skin was.
Whiter than hers. But that's not really surprising con-
sidering how fair he was while she, her hair inclined to
the brown. I think one may say so. To thee all flesh shall
come. How true, how true. And such flesh! Despatched.
No, I really am not very calm. Tea slopping in the saucer.
I hate mess, such clumsiness. It is uncharacteristic and
can only be put down to the deed. I have seen such mess
and worse in the canteen, which is why I refuse to eat
there. Besides, Mother always made such excellent sandwiches and I think I may say that I, too, am something
of a dab-hand.

49

Lord, have mercy,
Christ, have mercy,
Lord, have mercy.

What a pity that I never had the Latin. Mother always said. There was no excuse for it, she maintained. None. I can see her now. My Bernard should have the Latin, she said. He should have all the advantages of the other boys. The boys in 4A, I mean. What is he doing in 4B anyway, that is what I should like to know? 4B where you can't even get the Latin. But all her arguments were to no avail. And now it scarcely matters.

Dies irae

Thursday. I wonder if Thursday may be considered suitable for the Day of Wrath? Still, again, it was not of my choosing and nowhere have I heard it advanced that the Day shall occur on any specific day of the week. I suppose one would naturally tend to think in terms of a Sunday, but it was a Thursday they chose. Giggling in the outer office, thinking they were unobserved, unheard. He had his football practice, his work-out on Wednesdays. Keeping his body in trim for lust. Oh well, she said, pouting a little, I'll just have to stay in and wash my hair, that's all. And he touched her hair, saying something I could not hear. Some pretty compliment, no doubt, about her hair which would be, indeed was, fine and silky on Thursday morning. This morning. Perhaps that is what it means, anyway. Not a specific day of the week, and certainly not some sort of guessing game with God, but that we shall each meet our Day of Wrath at the appointed time. And theirs was appointed a Thursday. Dissolve the world in ashes. I wonder. How long will it take? The blaze will not go long undetected. The car to ashes, then, but not the flesh. No, I should definitely say not the flesh. Still, that is not promised. Charred perhaps, a little. But not, as one might say, incinerated. I imagine that, the blaze having been noticed, the fire brigade sent

for, they will, with their hoses and chemical foams, do all
in their power to save the bodies, for purposes of identification. That was a good touch, removing the number
plates. Just in case. The old man's car, he said, his hands
roaming her body. Thursday, I can get the old man's
car. The plates, safely at the bottom of the river, duly
weighted. To buy time, to delay discovery.

> How great a terror there will be
> when the Judge shall come
> who will thresh out everything thoroughly!

O how great the terror was. On their faces. When they
realised. Shock and embarrassment, I do believe. Clear
off, he said and would have said more had I not produced the gun, bringing it into the light of the torch and
levelling it at him. Funny, she turned to him for help,
clutching a scrap of cloth to her breasts. Such modesty!
The first and only time in her life, I should think. Yet
still her left breast was visible. Turned to *him* for help.
Amazing. But they were beyond help, anyway. He knew
it. But I, on the other hand, shall feel no terror when my
Judge shall come. None whatsoever. None. Fortitude, it
said on my report. Bernard shows great fortitude. That
pleased her, perhaps made up in some small measure for
the disappointment over the Latin. Funny how I always
kept the gun, cleaned and looked after it. A souvenir,
brought back from the war by my father. It was the war
that ruined your father, she always said, but somehow I
couldn't bring myself to part with this, his one souvenir.
And I always cleaned it, kept it ready. I think, towards
the end, her poor, lamented end, she had forgotten about
it, but I knew it would come in handy some day. This
day, as it happens. This Thursday of Wrath.

Tuba mirum
O I should like that. A trumpet sounding at my death.
It won't be possible, I suppose. One could, perhaps, write
it into one's will, but do they take notice of a 'prisoner's'

last wishes? For prisoner I shall be. Eventually. I have
known many – Aunt Lucy to name but one – who have
not respected the wishes of the dear departed. It amounts
to sacrilege in my book, Mother said, straight out, to
Lucy's face. If those were Henry's wishes, they should
have been abided by, to the letter. Well, she could die
easy on that score with me. To the letter, in every particular, I carried it out. If there is time, on Sunday, I
must take special flowers. A stone angel she wanted and
a stone angel she has got. Roses, I think. Or carnations.
She was particularly fond of carnations and though they
are a terrible price at the moment, she would not be-
grudge the cost since it is likely to be my last time. Well,
I could consult someone about the trumpet. If only she
were here, she'd know. It would require a codicil to the
will I have already made, but presumably that much at
least will be permitted me? I have already made arrangements for Mother's grave, of course. Upkeep and so on.
Though to make sure about the trumpet, perhaps I should
contact Bailey, Bailey and Simkins before they . . .

Mors stupebit
Ah, yes indeed they will stand amazed when I rise to
answer the Judge. I shall give a good account of myself.
And it is all here, written down in this notebook, pur-
chased from W. H. Smith and Son, specifically for the
purpose. There it all is, noted down. What they were
really like. So proud, she was, with her qualifications.
Three 'O' levels and excellent typing and dictation
speeds. And I've had experience, she said proudly, of
dictaphone work, should you require it. She'd had experience, all right. She proclaimed it with every twitch of
her hips, every pout of her lips. The way her eyes
swivelled to any man that entered the office. Sizing him
up, waiting her moment. The times I've caught her,
loitering in the corridors, talking and giggling with one
of the draughtsmen or one of those smart boys from
Accounts. He was a smart boy. Gregson himself told me.

I've got plans for that boy, he said. He'll get on. Go far. I don't intend to lose him to the competition. Yes, I said, but what about his morals? The look on his face, as though *I* had used a dirty word. What have morals got to do with it, he asked? Well, of course, you can't explain something like that to a man like Gregson and I could only bring myself to make the most general of complaints. Obliquely, of course. How could I say that I had seen him, his precious Brian, who was destined to go far, with his hand up my Brenda's skirt? They thought they were safe. They thought I knew nothing. But there are two entrances to my office. They didn't think of that, for all their qualifications. But then it is true that lust is blind. I would leave through her office and return via the draughtsmen's. The times I've heard her say, It's all right. He won't be back till two. On the dot. They laughed at my punctuality, although, on the whole, I did not figure much in their conversation. Such as it was, Filth in whispers, mostly. Him persuading. She putting up a pretence of resistance. It was on *that* they should have been judged, but Gregson thought only of efficiency. He did not care that they used the office as a brothel, provided their work was good. I asked permission to sack Brenda, thinking to nip it in the bud. But on what grounds? Her work is faultless. He talked a great deal about redundancy pay, the difficulties of being an employer these days. But then Gregson himself is not beyond reproach if all I hear of his behaviour at the Christmas parties is anything to go by. So I said nothing. Brenda remained, and although she did not cease to flirt with every man in the building, her most vile and special favours were reserved for Brian.

Judex ergo
The contralto voice. Always my favourite. Mother, in her day, possessed a fine contralto. She was universally acknowledged to be the prop and stay of the Christmas and

Easter performances of the *Messiah* in St Luke's Church Hall. How I thrilled to sit there, to hear her. Such firm, ringing tones. *He was despised. I* was despised. But no more. O no. No more. For when I say that Brenda flirted with every man in the building, that more than I would dare to number have put their hands on her body, I must note that *I* was the exception. With me, she behaved herself. And whenever I chose to interrupt their obscene trysts, Brian would always leap to his feet with a show of respect. Often, however, the hypocrisy of it was all too great since he would be at pains to adjust his dress in the sense of concealing his all too obvious excitement. It crossed my mind to suggest to him that he might wear looser trousers if it bothered him so much, but I knew it would be no use. Fashion before respectability. Of course. Naturally. Whatever is hidden shall be made manifest, indeed. And nothing shall remain unavenged. I have seen to that. I should have made some joke about it along these lines, but they would not have understood.

Quid sum, miser

I know well enough what I shall say. In addition to all that is written down here in my book. I regret now that I did not buy a more suitable-looking book. One with a dignified black cover, imitation leather, would have been more appropriate, but they were prohibitively expensive. I could not justify the expense to record the fumblings of a lout and a whore. I could all too easily imagine what Mother would have said. Yet now I wonder if this one, with its paper cover depicting green elephants might not be construed as a mark of disrespect to the Court? If there is time, perhaps I will buy another, one more suitable, and make a fair copy into it. Preserving the original, of course, to prove that I have not altered a word. There will be no one to plead for me. That is certain. I shall conduct my own defence. I shall produce my own evidence, read from this book, or the other if there is time to buy one and transcribe into it all that is written here. And I shall seek out the faces of their parents and of Gregson, of all who come who have mocked me behind my back. And in the parade of lust and obscenity which I shall conjure before them, they will understand what morals has to do with it!

Cum vix justus

I'm afraid. Such terrible words. Suddenly afraid. Get up. Don't listen. Carry the tea things into the kitchen. The words pursuing. Rattle the cup. Make more tea? Some of Mother's medicinal brandy. The last bottle, unfinished, still in the cupboard. Justifiable, surely, tonight of all nights? She would not object. Yes. Brandy. Not the proper glass. My hands tremble, clinking the bottle on this old tumbler which, if it should chip, or I should break it, would not matter. It is only one of the everyday glasses. Not Mother's best. Yes. Better now. Stinging, but warming. Was I then cold? I don't recall. The blaze was so hot, I had to retreat at once. Not just a matter of making good my escape, but to get away from the heat of the blazing car. Perhaps later, by the river, I caught a chill. Can't remember. It was certainly a cool evening, unseasonable for the time of year. As the Verger predicted. Yes, better now.

Rex tremendae

Such a wealth of noise. Exploding, rolling over me. I read that Mozart enjoyed the telling and hearing of filthy jokes. How then could he have written this? Dreadful majesty, indeed. It is not possible. If true, perhaps I should have chosen, tonight of all nights, the Verdi, for I know of no salacious caste to his mind. But I *prefer* the Mozart and probably the story is fabricated. Yes, yes. Tiny, tainted minds seeking to drag his greatness, his perfection, into the mire. As it has always been. O Fount of Pity. He will have pity on me. More than pity, Love.

Welcome. For I have done His work. I set out to do it
and it is – I believe I may in all humility say this – well
done. *Salva me, fons pietatis.* I do not have the Latin,
nor did I ever learn to sing in tune. On that count,
Mother was always impatient with me, but then it is said
that she had perfect pitch and it must have been irritating
for her. Even painful. The prop and stay of the local
Operatic Society, although it was in Oratorio that she
excelled. And she would have been so proud, had I been
a choirboy at St Luke's.

Recordare
Yes, recall. The day she wore white stockings, giving her
the air of a little girl. A Novice, even. They were stockings, not tights. For later I saw them. She leaning, sprawl-
ing back across the desk. His hand pushing up her skirt
to show the obscene worm of black suspender holding up
the white stocking. Exploring with his hand. Giggling,
No, stop it, in that voice which lies, encourages, demands
that he go on, go further. Recall that I saw this and
recalled all that I had been taught, all that I *knew* to be
right. And I knew then, like a revelation – I believe the
word may be permitted – that I, for whose poor and
undeserving sake, He had died, could not stand by and
witness without raising my voice and, yes, my arm. I
could not alone stop the World's rot, but I could take a
stand, make an example of them, secure for myself the
secular pulpit of the Court from which to bear witness.
Had I had the Latin it might have been possible for me
to enter the Church, to serve God and my Blessed Saviour
in the cloth. But by then it was too late. And I've never
been one for Theology as such. Those guessing games
with God. Besides, Mother needed me. Work had to be
found, money brought in. My duty was clear and I do
not regret it. Besides, I have been a Sidesman for many
years now, and that, too, is service which He will not
overlook. He who absolved Mary Magdalene and heard

the prayer of the thief, will certainly give me redemption. If she, like Mary Magdalene, had shown one sign, one timid gesture of repentance, it would have been possible to spare her. Piss off, you dirty old bastard, she shouted when she saw me. Her breasts, her naked breasts wobbled with the force of her voice. And he, poised above her, stared at me as though I was mad. They scrambled apart, she sitting up, clutching her blouse or something to her breasts. Do something, she said, as though he hadn't done enough. O I blushed then, but not now. I do not groan as one guilty. He groaned, when he saw her breast smashed by the bullet, the first, perfectly placed. A neat hole in that pap, in her heart. Blood oozing. O Christ, he groaned. A profanity. The only time that Blessed name ever passed his lips, I dare say. O I shall be judged, all right, but not by Him. Yet I must beware of the sin of pride. I confess it. I *am* proud of this day's work, but my pride is that of a Soldier of Christ, not of a worthless man. Or the surely justifiable pride of a man who, in humility, has rid the World of filth. Only a speck, admittedly, but all that one man may reasonably do. It will be taken into account. I shall be placed among the sheep. On Thy right hand. While mine are steadier now.

Confutatis Maledictis
His skin was so white. He looked bemused, his mouth hanging open, looked from her body to my face. Frozen, he was. Unable to move. I could perhaps, then, have hesitated, had pity on him, but I saw that, still, despite the shock of my intrusion, despite Brenda's swift and beautiful death, he remained aroused. A ram, a goat, half-kneeling on the back seat, over her. I hesitated no longer. That's where I shot him first, knowing it would not kill. A third bullet to despatch him. I was very close then. It was not clean and neat like her death had been. Bone and face splitting. His hands down there, too late, to protect what, no doubt, he prided himself on. For that was the best of him, I have no doubt. A man of only one

57

part. Damned and confounded. And then the fire, to reduce them to ashes, to begin here what they will suffer for eternity.

Lacrimosa

So why, why am I weeping? Not since Mother went. Not once. Now, suddenly, tears. Splashing and blurring. I must not get my notebook wet. Must not. Push it away, knock over the glass. Empty. The brandy. Yes, of course. Maudlin. Not used to it, alcohol. Only to steady the nerves. I have not sinned. I have nothing to weep about. It is not true that I . . . coveted . . . her. O I know that's what they said. I know it. Jealous old git. Those smart young men with their smiles and their tight trousers. That's what they said when I chased them off. Brenda has work to do, I'd say. And no doubt you have, too. Staring down the front of her dress, bending over her. O I finished ages ago, she'd say, cool as you please. Then come into my office and bring your pad. And they thought it was because I wanted her for myself. I wanted to save her. Once I tried. I did. I tried. I begged her. She said there was no harm in it. Then she told me to mind my own business. I could have had her sacked for that. Insubordination. And he, Brian, became bolder, from which I understood that she had told him of our conversation. I did want to save her and to make her understand that the filth these young men muttered when I sent them packing was only the sickness of their narrow minds by which they sought to contaminate me. I'm only interested, I told her, in your welfare. You're a pretty girl, good at your job. I'm only interested in your purity. If I could only bring you to Christ. I want to make you understand that only by keeping yourself pure can you be happy, and assured of Salvation. I wrote it all down afterwards in my book. For she condemned herself. She laughed. It's a bit late for that, she said. And laughed. And I knew then that I would kill her. That I would kill her in her obscenity with him, with the one she had chosen. I knew it had to be. So why, why am I weeping? Lean back, close the eyes. A good cry is good for you, they say. Nothing like a good cry and a cup of tea, Mother always used to say. And prayer, of course. Take Thou my ending into Thy care. Such comfort. And yet when? That is all I regret. They will not take me out and hang me. For that I *could* weep. It was a disgrace, Mother said, when they abolished the death penalty. She wrote to our MP but did not receive a satisfactory reply. I agreed with her then and now more so than ever, for they will delay my coming, my reward. I have very great admiration for that man in America who demanded his own execution. I am weeping because it cannot be so for me. The record has stopped and in the sudden silence, I can hear the sound of my own weeping.

Domine Jesu
I kneel down to turn the record over. It is not necessary to kneel down but somehow easier. You worship that gramophone, Mother said. Yet it was she who taught me to love music. I am careful not to let any stray tears fall on the shiny black surface of the record. Kneeling. In prayer. I should pray. God, see this deed I have done. God bless my Mother. God, let me come to you in glory. Be *pleased* with me. There is a balm in the music. Better now. Much better. A little unsteady on my legs from kneeling. Perhaps Mother was right after all. The record player *is* at an inconvenient height. Being handy about the house I could build a new shelf for it, higher. But where would be the point now? More brandy. Just a drop. I'm calmer now. Excited even. It is not every day a man can truly point to a deed well done. After I spoke to Brenda, pleaded with her to see the error of her ways, Brian became bolder, though not overtly so. A certain slowness in rising when I entered the office. He left, went about his business at his own, insolent pace. There was no point in complaining to Gregson. None whatsoever. I

bided my time. It was obvious that they carried on outside the office. There was, consequently, less overt activity within the office. A kiss or two. His hand on her breast, but I could hear them plotting, making arrangements. I wrote it all down. Mondays she baby-sat for her married sister. He, of course, joined her. How I feared for those innocent babes, left in the charge of such creatures! I did not dare to think, to imagine what, on some settee no doubt, they would get up to. Tuesdays they met, but without any specific, regular plan. Sometimes I would understand that they had been to a cinema, or a public house. Wednesdays was for keeping his body trim, when he prepared himself for her, making lewd jokes with other smart young men, no doubt, while she washed her hair. Thursdays . . . Thursday was the Day of Wrath.

Sed signifer
Now I can see them standing in the light. A blazing light. Unimaginable, really. Naked, of course. A light so strong and burning on their nakedness, their lusts that every imperfection, blot and stain is revealed at last. Will she cover her breasts before the Lord, I wonder? Will he seek to hide the bloody pulp of his sex? Like Adam and Eve, will they at last recognise their shame?

Quam olim Abrahae
Such a fine chorus. Stirring. As was promised to Abraham and his seed. They knew about seed, all right. All they ever knew about. The spilling of seed. Which is, of course, a mortal sin. O such music lifts the heart and soul. *Quam olim Abrahae la-da-da-da.* It is a curse not being able to sing in tune. Mother might have taken more pains to teach me. But no, no. Forgive me. She saw in me no natural talent and you cannot foster what is not there. The seeds of music, to force the metaphor a little, were not there to germinate. You were made to appreciate, Bernard, not to perform, she said. And she was right. I

have appreciation. I could appreciate them for what they truly were. I could discern the seeds of evil in them. It was my unhappy lot to see them flower and blossom. I went once – I put it in my notebook – to his desk. It was a hot day. She was half-naked. He, I knew, would be sunning himself, shirtless, in the park with her and others of their ilk. I went to his office and made a cursory examination of his desk. In the bottom drawer, inevitably, I found filth. A magazine, no doubt passed around the office, shared among those bright young men with their qualifications and ambitions. Women with splayed legs and bulbous breasts. I was sickened to look at it. Like that time, years ago, when that boy Young brought to school magazines of a similar nature and made me look. I didn't understand the words he and his cronies used and when they explained to me, I felt defiled. But if ever evidence was needed of the way the World has gone, it may be found in the comparison of those magazines. Strange, how clearly I remember them . . . The ones borrowed from Young's elder brother were – if such a word may be used at all in such a context – positively modest compared to that which, trembling, I took from his desk and secreted in a brown envelope. When I told Mother about the magazines Young had made me look at, she was very kind. She made me understand that chastity was the only way. I swore a vow then and have never, ever broken it. That other magazine, that obscenity I shall produce as evidence of the sort of degenerate he was.

Hostias

Put it out of mind. Make offerings, sacrifices of prayers and praise. Yes. A World rid of such filth. Why could they not understand the beauty of the world, the comfort and safety of faith? Yet how could Christ enter into such foetid souls? I had watched them before. I did not act rashly. Thursdays, invariably, he could borrow his father's car and they found – I heard them discussing it – a place on the Common where they thought they were private. Not your Lover's Lane. O no. For them a little track that ran into the woods that skirt the Common, near the old machine factory, now derelict, where boys have scrawled obscenities and crude drawings on the walls. Sometimes they left the car. Sometimes they did it on God's good earth. Her skirts about her waist. His trousers open only for convenience. But they became bolder. I invested some of Mother's money in a pair of binoculars. It was a great deal of money, but I can justify the expenditure. For I knew then, when I bought them, that I was God's instrument, that Mother would understand. I had made few inroads on her small bequest and all, I feel, can safely say, in the cause of Good. I had to be sure. I had to give them time to mend their ways. But all the evidence was conclusive. They were damned beyond redemption on this earth. I could only save them by killing them, you see.

Sanctus

I made one last appeal to her. Subtly, of course. May we, I said, with just a touch of irony in my tone, May we expect to hear of your engagement soon? She looked at me as though I had gone off my head. No. Why? She was genuinely surprised. Give her that. She did not dissemble. To my shame I stumbled a little. I thought, I said, you seem to be . . . you and young Brian . . . She laughed. I'm not going to tie myself down to any man, she said. Not me. Not for years yet. I've seen too many girls ruin their lives. O no. I want to live a little first. I dismissed her, for I could not bear her presence near me. I had seen her, only the night before, performing . . . things, acts . . . with him . . . Acts which would not even be acceptable between a man and his lawful wedded wife. But she had no intention, nor he of . . . I was very upset that day. I told Gregson I was unwell and came home. I took out the gun and cleaned it. I loaded it. I felt so strong then, so proud. I gave thanks. I experienced one of those precious moments which are the blessing of all true believers. I knelt and gave thanks, gave promise, my hands clasped around the heavy metal of the gun. My heart was bursting with joy. I had dedicated myself and I knew the familiar words to be truer than ever. They seemed full of life and meaning. Vibrant. I spoke aloud, nursing the gun. Heaven and earth *are* full of Thy glory, I said. I could feel it. And knowing it only made their sin the greater. It was unbearable, like a shadow passing over the sun, darkening the glorious earth.

Benedictus
I felt blessed. I bicycled to the Common that Tuesday evening and, after having chained my bicycle to the usual tree – one cannot be too careful these days – I walked until nightfall. I knew I would not encounter them. My mood of ecstatic comprehension of and communion with my God softened with the walking but words, these words, lulled in my head, over and over. Blessed is he that cometh in the name of the Lord. I felt as though a soft radiance surrounded me. If there is one moment in my life which I would choose to relive, it would be that moment. I watched the people on the Common. People walking their dogs. Youths playing football, whirling those brightly-coloured plastic discs through the air. Beautiful. Blessed is he that cometh in the name of the Lord. As night fell they dispersed, leaving me alone. I looked up at the sky. There was no moon, but the stars were bright and clear. Voices fading. A few late people scurrying home across the Common. Such peace. Such certainty. I lifted up my head and contemplated the Universe. I spread my arms in welcome and gratitude. Hosanna in the highest! I wanted to shout it but, mindful of what people might think, I and God had to make do with a whisper. I knew, however, that He would

63

understand and accept my whisper. I had obtained a state of grace. I cycled home and slept deeply, without the aid of my pill. For the first time since Mother was taken, I did not require the pill to make me sleep. Wasn't that a sign in itself? The end to a perfect day, I said to myself as I dropped off. Blessed is he that cometh in the name of the Lord.

Agnus Dei
They didn't notice a thing, of course. My calm, my gentleness born of certainty, the outward show of my purpose. To them I was unchanged. She took dictation in her white stockings, typed my letters and did the filing. I smiled when she brought my morning coffee. He was like a peacock. A new shirt, black, splashed with blood. No, roses. Red roses. Like blood. Without a tie, of course. Showing half of his chest, that body he nurtured and pampered like a woman's. And I heard that it would be all right for Thursday. I almost clapped my hands with glee. All day there was a kind of excitement in me. In the evening I went to Church and knelt for a long time in the cool solace of prayer. Later I scrubbed my body clean. Checked the gun again. Only yesterday? It seems so long ago. Lamb of God that takest away the sins of the world. Always my favourite prayer. Always. And it is not presumptious of me to say that I was the lamb of God then. I was going to take away the sins of the world. Some of them, anyway. I met the Verger as I left and he, glancing up at the sky, assured me that the good weather would break. This alarmed me. I had counted on a fine evening, one when they would venture out of the car. But I put the thought out of my mind. I knew that there would be a way. I took a pill, though, to be quite certain of sleep. I wanted to be fresh, alert, ready for any contingency. I did not feel that this was a failure, that I had lost my state of grace. It was only natural that I should be excited, restless, anxious to do it now, at last.

Lux aeterna

They did not arrive until late. The weather *had* changed.
It did not rain, but the wind was waving the tops of the
trees about and had a distinct chill to it. Perhaps that
was when I caught cold? I came close to despair, thinking they would not come. But they did come, at dusk.
For a moment, as she got out of the car, she stared into
the trees, straight towards me. He leaned over to open the
back door for her. She ignored the door, staring towards
me. I could not hear him speak, but no doubt he urged
her to hurry. It was funny the way she paused, looked
towards me, as though she knew, or sensed something.
She got into the back of the car and closed the door. He
got in beside her, from the other side and their bodies
blurred together into one, awful flesh. Later he opened
the window, wound it right down. I knew it was a sign.
His skin was so white in the falling darkness. I knew then
that he was naked, that the time had come. I crept forward so quietly they did not suspect a thing. I stood
listening to their murmurs. Filth. Not words. The moans
of the damned. I turned on my torch, swamping them
with light. My particular eternal light, I suppose one
might say. Then I killed them. She through the breast.
He in the groin, then the head which split open. Afterwards, I was too busy to think. Only when I had fled the
blaze and thrown the registration plates into the river did
I feel a sense of anti-climax. I came back here, knowing
that even the pills would not enable me to sleep tonight.
Put on the record, made some tea. And now it is already
Friday, the day after the Day of Wrath. The record
player hums. The gun, with three shots fired, lies on top
of the notebook, into which is tucked the obscene pub-
lication I took from his desk. Everything is ready. I wonder how long it will be before there is a knock on the
door? How long before they find me? I shall, of course,
offer absolutely no resistance. There remains only the
problem of whether I should delay, buy a new notebook

and copy out my evidence. For if they do not come for me, I had thought to give myself up. But the notebook does bother me. Green elephant's really aren't suitable. All in all, now that it is done, I think I was wrong. I should have bought the black one, even though it was expensive. It would have been more fitting. But perhaps it won't matter? For Thou art merciful and will forgive such trifles. In a moment, perhaps, I shall get up and play the record again. I don't like the silence. The humming silence of the record player, the empty house. I think, perhaps, for the first time I am afraid. Weakness. My Mother always said that was my fault. I was weak, didn't try hard enough to get on in the world. I must not be weak now. There are many small things to be done. Put the cap back on the brandy bottle. Wash up the cup, saucer, spoon and glass. Replace the brandy bottle in the correct place. Turn the record over again, wipe it free of dust, place the needle gently, carefully on the edge, to avoid scratching. And then I can listen again. It always helps, the music. Soothes the timid as well as the savage breast. Yes. Yes, that's what I must do. In a minute. And then soon I will be in the pulpit of the Court, making my speech. There will be a stenographer to take it all down, every word, on one of those silent typewriters. Reporters scribbling away in shorthand, as Brenda used to do. I will scrutinise the faces of their families and friends and watch as they understand how they have failed, are to blame in spawning their sinful children. I shall lay blame where it belongs, for they are, when all is said and done, only an example. From them I shall argue to the parents and all the staff, to Gregson himself and outwards to the schoolteachers and the television people and the whole of Society. My voice will rise on a note of controlled passion and I shall cry, at the end, in ringing tones: *Mea culpa. Mea maxima culpa. Requiem aeternam dona eis. Domine: et lux perpetua luceat eis.* They will respect me then, not knowing that I have it by rote,

66

from the leaflet inserted in the record sleeve, but thinking that I have the Latin which is, after all, the language of the Law as well as of God. *Requiem aeternam*, I will shout. And then, O then, I shall not be so miserably cold and afraid. Surely?

Antonia Fraser

DEATH OF AN OLD DOG

Paulina Gavin came back from the vet with a sweet expression on her heart-shaped face. The little crease which sometimes – just slightly – marred the smooth white skin between her brows was absent. Her eyes, grey yet soft, swept round the sitting room. Then they came to rest, lovingly, on Richard.

'Darling, I'm late! But supper won't be late. I've got it all planned.'

Widowhood had made of Richard Gavin a good, as well as a quick cook. But Paulina had not seen fit to call on his talents before her visit to the vet: he found no note of instructions awaiting him. Now Paulina kissed him with delicious pressure on his cheek, just where his thick grizzled sideburn ended. It was her special place.

From this, Richard knew that Ibo was condemned to die.

Viewing the situation with detachment, as befitting a leading barrister, Richard was not the slightest bit surprised that the verdict should have gone against Ibo. The forces ranged against each other were simply not equal. On the one side, the vet, in his twenties, and Paulina, not much older. On the other side, Ibo. And Ibo was not merely old. He was a very old dog indeed.

He dated from the early days of Richard's first marriage, and that balmy period not only seemed a great while since, a long, long time ago (in the words of Richard's favourite quotation from Ford) but actually was. Even the origin of the nickname Ibo was lost in

68

some private joke of his marriage to Grace : as far as he could remember the dog had begun as Hippolytus. Was it an allusion to his sympathies in the Nigerian Civil War? Based on the fact that Ibo, like the Biafrans, was always starving. . . . That too seemed a long, long time ago.

You could therefore say sentimentally that Ibo and Richard had grown old together. Except that it would not actually be true. For Richard had gingerly put out one toe towards middle age, only to be dragged backwards by Paulina's rounded arms, her curiously strong little hands. And having been rescued, Richard was obviously reposited in the prime of life, as though on a throne.

His past athletic prowess (including a really first-class tennis game which only pressure at the Bar had prevented him taking further) was easy to recall, looking at his tall, trim figure. If anything, he had lost weight recently. And it was not only the endearing Paulina but Richard's friends who generally described him as 'handsomer than ever'. It was as though the twenty-five-year age gap between Richard and his second wife had acted upon him as a rejuvenating injection.

The same miracle had not been performed for the master's dog. Casting his mind back, Richard could dimly recall embarrassing walks in the park with Ibo, portrait of a young dog at the evident height of his amorous powers. Now the most desirable spaniel bitch would flaunt herself in vain before him. Like Boxer in *Animal Farm*, where energy was concerned, Ibo was merely a shadow of his former self. And he did not even have Boxer's tragic dignity. Ibo by now was just a very shaggy, and to face the facts fully, a very smelly old dog.

Richard stirred in his chair. The topic must be raised. Besides, he had another important subject to discuss with Paulina, sooner or later.

'How did you get on at the vet, darling?' he called. She had after all not yet mentioned her visit.

But Paulina, having skipped into her kitchen, apparently did not hear. Pre-arranged odours were wafting from it. Richard guessed that she would soon emerge having removed her apron. He guessed that she would be bearing with her a bottle of red wine, already opened, and two glasses on a tray. There was, he suspected, a strong possibility that supper would be eaten by candle-light.

Both guesses were correct. The suspicion was confirmed when Paulina artlessly discovered some candles left over from Christmas and decided on impulse to use them up.

'Why not? Just for us,' she enquired to no one in par-ticular, as she sat down at the now positively festive little table with its browny-red casserole, its red Beaujolais and scarlet candles. Then Paulina's manner quite changed.

'Poor Ibo,' sighed Paulina, 'I'm afraid the vet didn't hold out much hope.'

'Hope?' repeated Richard in a surprised voice. It was not surely a question of *hope* – what hope could there possibly be for a very old, very smelly dog – but of life. It was the continuation of Ibo's life they were discussing, for that was all he had to expect, not the possibility of his magical rejuvenation.

'Well, *hope*,' repeated Paulina in her turn, sounding for the first time ruffled, as though the conversation had taken an unexpected and therefore unwelcome turn. 'Hope is so important, isn't it? Without hope, I don't see much point in any of us going on – '

But Richard's attention was distracted. There was an absence. He would have noticed it immediately had it not been for Paulina's charade with the dinner.

Where was Ibo? Obese, waddling, grey-muzzled, fre-quently flea-ridden, half-blind, where was Ibo? Normally his first action on entering the sitting room would have been to kiss, no slobber over, Richard's hand. Then Ibo, an optimist, might have wagged his stumpy tail as though despite the lateness of the hour and his incapacity, a walk was in the offing. Finally, convinced of his own absurdity, he would have made for the fire, pausing for a last lick of

Richard's hand. None of this had happened. Where was Ibo?

Paulina began to speak quickly, muttering things about further tests, the young vet's kindness, the need to take a dispassionate decision, and so forth, which all seemed to add up to the fact that the vet had kept the dog in overnight. Once again Richard cut in.

'You do realise Toddie comes home from school tomorrow?'

This time an expression of sheer panic crossed Paulina's face. It was only too obvious she had quite forgotten.

'How can he be?' she began, 'he's only just gone there – ' She stopped. She had remembered. Toddie, the strange silent ten-year-old son of Richard's first marriage, was returning the next day from school to have his new plate tightened. The dentist had emphasised that the appointments had to be regular, and had thus overruled protests from Richard who wanted Toddie to wait for half-term. At first Toddie had taken the news of his quick turn round with his usual imperturbability. But after a moment he had suddenly knelt down and flung his arms round Ibo, a mat of fur before the fire.

'Then I'll be seeing you very soon again, won't I, you good old boy? The best dog in the world.' It was a long speech for Toddie.

Toddie's embraces were reserved exclusively for Ibo. His father had tried a few grave kisses after Grace's death. Toddie held himself rigid as though under attack. Later they had settled for ritual handshakes. When Richard married Paulina he had advised her against any form of affectionate assault on Toddie, warned by his own experiences. For Paulina, the frequent light kiss was as natural a mode of communication as Richard's solemn handshake. Baulked of this, she had ended up deprived of any physical contact at all with Toddie. At first it worried her : a motherless boy. . . . Later, as her step-son remained taciturn, not so much a motherless boy as an inscrutable person, she was secretly glad she was not committed to hugging and kissing this enigma with his unsmiling lips, and disconcertingly expressionless eyes.

Only two things provoked any kind of visible reaction from Toddie. One was crime, murder to be precise. No doubt it was a natural concomitant to his father's career. But Paulina sometimes found the spectacle of Toddie poring over the newspapers in search of some gruesome trial rather distasteful. It was true that he concentrated on the law reports, showing for example considerable knowledge of appeal procedure, rather than on the horror stories in the popular press. Perhaps he would grow up to be a barrister like Richard. . . . In which case, where murder was concerned, he was making a flying start.

Toddie's other visible interest was of course Ibo.

Jolted by the prospect of the boy's return, Paulina now launched into a flood of explanation concerning the true nature of Ibo's condition. Ibo had a large growth, said the vet. Hadn't they noticed it? Richard clenched his hands. How long since he had brought himself to examine Ibo? Ibo simply existed. Or had simply existed up to the present time. Paulina went on to outline the case, extremely lucidly, for 'putting Ibo out of his misery' as she phrased it. Or rather to be honest, sparing him the misery that was to come. Nobody pretended that Ibo was in violent misery now, a little discomfort perhaps. But he would shortly *be* in misery, that was the point. Richard listened calmly and without surprise. Had he not known since the moment that his wife pressed her lips to his cheek that Ibo was condemned to die?

What Richard Gavin had not realised, and did not realise until he conceded, judicially, regretfully, the case for Ibo's demise, was that the old dog was not actually condemned to die. He was already dead. Had been dead throughout all the fairly long discussion. Had been put to sleep by the vet that very afternoon on the authority, the sole authority, of Paulina Gavin. Who had then returned audaciously, almost flirtatiously, to argue her senior

and distinguished husband round to her own point of view. . . .

The look on the face of Richard Gavin, Q.C., was for one instant quite terrible. But Paulina held up her own quite bravely. With patience – she was not nearly so frightened of Richard now as she had been when they first married – she pointed out to her husband the wisdom and even kindness of her strategy. Someone had to make the decision, and so she, Paulina, had made it. In so doing, she had removed from Richard the hideous, the painful necessity of condemning to death an old friend, a dear old friend. It was easier for her – Richard had after all known Ibo for so much longer. Yet since Richard was such a rational man and loved to think every decision through, she had felt she owed it to him to argue it all out.

'Confident of course that you would make your case?'

Richard's voice sounded guarded, as his voice did sometimes in court, during a cross-examination. His expression was quite blank : for a moment he reminded Paulina uncomfortably of Toddie. But she stuck firmly to her last.

'I know I was right, darling,' she said, 'I acted for the best. You'll see. Someone had to decide.'

There remained the problem of Toddie's precipitate return, the one factor which, to be honest, Paulina had left out of her calculations. She had expected to be able to break the sad news at half-term, a decent interval away. But the next morning, Paulina, pretty as a picture in a gingham house-dress at breakfast, made it clear that she could cope with that too. With brightness she handed Richard his mail :

'*Personal and Confidential!* Is it the bank?'

With brightness she let it be understood that it was she, Paulina, who would sacrifice her day at the office – the designers' studio she ran with such *élan* – to ferry Toddie to and from school. Although she had already sacrificed an afternoon going to the vet. The only thing Richard was expected to do, Paulina rattled on, was to return from *his* office, in other words his chambers, in the afternoon and tell his son the news about the dog.

Richard continued to wear his habitual morning expression, a frown apparently produced by his mail :

'No, it's not the bank,' he said.

'Income Tax, then?' Paulina was determined to make conversation.

'No.'

'Some case, I suppose.'

'You could put it like that.'

'Why here? Why not to your chambers?' Paulina carried on chattily.

'Paulina,' said Richard, pushing back his chair and rising. 'You must understand that I don't exactly look forward to telling Toddie that Ibo is dead.'

'Oh God, darling,' cried Paulina, jumping up in her turn, her eyes starting with bright tears, 'I know, I know, I *know*.' She hugged all that was reachable of his imposing figure. 'But it was for *him*.'

'For Ibo?'

'Yes, for him. That poor dear old fellow. Poor, poor old Ibo. I know, I understand. It's the saddest thing in the world, the death of an old dog. But it is – somehow, isn't it, darling? – inevitable.'

The hugging came to an end, and then Paulina dried her tears. Richard went off to his study, the large book-lined room which Paulina had created for him above the garage. He indicated that he would telephone his clerk with a view to taking the whole day off from his chambers.

One of the features of the study was a large picture window which faced out at the back over the fields to the wood. To protect Richard's privacy, the study had no windows overlooking the house. There was merely a brick façade. This morning, Paulina suddenly felt that both the study and Richard were turning their back on her,

74

But that was fanciful. She was overwrought on account of poor Toddie. And of course poor Ibo.

Paulina reminded herself that she too was not without her feelings, her own fondness for the wretched animal. It had been a brave and resolute thing she had done to spare Richard, something of which she would not have been capable a few years back. How much the studio had done for her self-confidence! Nerves calmed by the contemplation of her new wise maturity, Paulina got the car out of the garage and went off to fetch Toddie.

Of course Toddie knew something was wrong the moment he entered the empty house. He slipped out of the car and ran across the courtyard the moment they returned; although by re-parking the car in the garage immediately, Paulina had hoped to propel him straight into his father's care. As it was, she refused to answer Toddie's agitated question as to why Ibo did not come to greet him. She simply took him by the shoulder and led him back as fast as possible to the garage. Then it was up the stairs and into the study. Paulina did not intend to linger. She had no wish to witness the moment of Toddie's breakdown.

She had once asked Richard how Toddie took the news of his mother's death, so sudden, so appalling, in a road accident on the way to pick him up at kindergarten.

'He howled,' Richard replied.

'You mean, cried and cried.'

'No, howled. Howled once. One terrible howl, then nothing. Just as if someone had put their hand across his mouth to stop him. It was a howl like a dog.'

Paulina shuddered. It was a most distasteful comparison to recall at the present moment. She was by now at the head of the narrow staircase and thrusting Toddie into the big book-lined room with its vast window. But before she could leave, Richard was saying in that firm voice she recognised from the courts:

'Toddie, you know about the law, don't you?'

The boy nodded and stared.

'Well, I want you to know that there has been a trial here. The trial of Ibo.' Toddie continued to stare, his large round eyes almost fish-like, Paulina turned and fled away down the stairs. No doubt Richard knew his own business – and his own son – best. But to her it sounded a most ghoulish way of breaking the news.

A great deal of time passed; time enough for Paulina to speak several times to her office (pleasingly incapable of managing without her); time enough for Paulina to reflect how very unused she had become to a housewife's enforced idleness, waiting on the movements of the males of the family. She tried to fill the gap by making an interesting tea for Toddie, in case that might solace him. But it was in fact long past tea-time when Paulina finally received some signal from the study across the way. She was just thinking that if Richard did not emerge soon, she would be late returning Toddie to Graybanks (and that would hardly help him to recover) when the bleep-bleep of the intercom roused her.

'He's coming down,' said Richard's voice, slightly distorted by the wire which crackled. 'Naturally he doesn't want to talk about it. So would you take him straight back to school? As soon as possible. No, no tea thank you. He'll be waiting for you in the car.' And that was all. The intercom clicked off.

Upset, in spite of herself, by Richard's brusqueness, Paulina hastily put away the interesting tea as best she could. Still fighting down her feelings, she hurried to put on her jacket and re-cross the courtyard. But she could not quite extinguish all resentment. It was lucky, she thought crossly, that as Richard grew older he would have a tactful young wife at his elbow; that should preserve him from those slight rigidities, or perhaps acidities was a better word, to which all successful men were prone after a certain age. For the second time that day she recalled with satisfaction the moral courage she had shown in having Ibo put down on her own initiative without distressing her husband; there was no doubt that Richard was relying on her already.

This consciousness of virtue enabled her – but only just – to stifle her irritation at the fact that Richard had not even bothered to open the big garage doors for her. Really, men were the most ungrateful creatures; it was she, not Richard, who was facing a cross-country journey in the dark; he might at least have shown his normal chivalry to ease her on her way – taking back his son, not hers, to school. Reliance was one thing, dependence and over-dependence quite another. Still in an oddly perturbed mood for one normally so calm and competent, Paulina slipped through the little door which led to the garage.

She went towards the car. She was surprised that the engine was already running. And Toddie was not in the passenger seat. In fact the car appeared to be empty. She tried the door. It was locked. Behind her was the noise of the little side-door shutting.

About the same time Richard Gavin was thinking that he would miss Paulina, he really would: her cooking, her pretty ways, her office gossip. Habit had even reconciled him to the latter. In many ways she had been a delightful even a delicious wife for a successful man. The trouble was that she clearly would not make any sort of wife for an older man dying slowly and probably painfully of an incurable disease. This morning the doctors had finally given him no hope. He had been waiting for the last hope to vanish, putting off the moment, before sharing the fearful burden with her.

Really, her ruthless and overbearing behaviour over poor Ibo had been a blessing in disguise. For it had opened his eyes just in time. No, Paulina would certainly not be the kind of wife to solace her husband's protracted deathbed. She might even prove to be the dreadful sort of person who believed in euthanasia 'to put him out of his misery'. He corrected himself. Paulina might even *have* proved to be such a person.

Back in the garage, the smell of exhaust fumes soon began to fill the air. Still no one came to open the garage doors. Even the side-door was now apparently locked from the outside. Paulina's last conscious thought, fighting in vain to get the garage doors open, was that she would really have to arrange automatic openers one of these days – now that Richard was no longer as young as he was, no longer eager to help her.

A couple of fields away, in a copse, Toddie was showing his father the exact spot where he would like to have Ibo buried. Richard had been quite desperate, as he would tell the police later, to cheer the poor little chap up. It was a natural, if sentimental expedition for a father to make with his son. A son so bereft by the death of an old dog. A son so early traumatised by the death of his mother (a step-mother was not at all the same thing, alas).

And when the police came, as they surely would, to the regrettable conclusion that the second Mrs Gavin's death had not in fact been an accident, well, it really all added up, didn't it? Exactly the same factors came into play and would be ably, amply, interminably examined by the long list of child psychiatrists to whom Toddie would be inevitably subjected.

But Toddie, Richard reflected with a certain professional detachment, would be more than a match for them. What interested him most about his son was his burning desire to get on with the business of confessing his crime. He seemed to be positively looking forward to his involvement with the police and so forth. He was certainly very satisfied with the way he had compassed his step-mother's death.

Richard was also quite surprised at the extent of Toddie's knowledge of the law concerning murderers. You could almost say that Toddie had specialised in the subject. Whereas he himself had never had much to do with that line of country. Richard realised suddenly that it was the first time he had ever really felt interested by his son.

78

Under the circumstances, Toddie very much doubted that he would have to spend many years in prison. He intended to end up as a model prisoner. But there might have to be a bad patch from which he could be redeemed : otherwise he might not present an interesting enough case, and the interesting cases always got out first. No, Toddie really had it all worked out.

'Besides, Dad,' ended Toddie, no longer in the slightest bit taciturn, 'I'm proud of what I did. You told me how to do it. But I'd have done it somehow anyway. She deserved to die. She condemned Ibo to death without telling us. Behind our backs. No proper trial. And killed him. Ibo, the best dog in the world.'

Reg Gadney

THE DEMOCRATIC MURDER

Adultery is the application of democracy to love.
H. L. Mencken

Blood had drenched everything. His shoes squelched in it.
A great red stain covered his shirt like some geographer's
idea of an ocean on a map. It stuck his fingers together
like a setting glue and still it dripped off the knife in his
hand. So when the college porter came into his office,
saw the two students dead on the floor with Carlo holding the bloodied knife and heard the whisper, 'I didn't
do it,' he replied, 'Like bloody hell, you didn't . . .' and
ran for his life to the nearest telephone. But, of course,
those worthy men in civilian blue uniforms most often
see people come and go. They don't always know what's
gone on before or even in between while. Yet this was a
terrible way to end the college year : a part-time visiting
Tutor standing there with the blood of students, quite
literally, on his hands. The man was obviously a maniac.

You could have been forgiven for thinking that about
Carlo Fortismere. His face looked like a reflection in a
spoon : pushed, pulled and melancholy. On first sight
you'd have put him somewhere between twenty and
forty : either a man preparing for middle age with a
modest diet and the easy life or a young man of intem-
perate habits. The appearance was a doubtful one. The
clothes were almost fashionable. A Jermyn Street shirt
from the New Year sales. Pressed blue jeans and expensive shoes. The style suggested irresponsibility : it was
hard to place. One drew the conclusion that here was one
of life's confident and more experienced tricksters.

Jane Calderton had surprised everyone by introducing Carlo to the college. She spoke up at a staff and student meeting which was something she never usually did by saying: 'I propose Carlo Fortismere, Sci-Fi novelist, as Visiting Tutor.' Her little speech was delivered hesitantly, with a slight stammer in fact, in the sort of upper class accent you rarely heard amongst painting students at the time. Staff and students listened with the respect a stammer often commands. She said Fortismere had a vision of the future, imagination, eloquence; that he was young, just the 'sort of new blood we all need'. In so far as the only other candidate for selection as a gesture to what the college called 'participatory democracy' was the leader of a Punk Rock Group who anyway had told the college, the country and the world to get stuffed, Carlo's election was passed unanimously. Thus, that year, he enjoyed the benefit of part-time employment as a teacher of painting unhampered by a single conventional qualification for the job. 'I'm approaching my beginning . . .' he said to the students. By which he meant forty years of age. 'From the wrong side.' By which he meant he'd just passed forty, adding 'Comrades'. By which he meant they were neither his comrades nor his acquaintances. The students loved it. Carlo didn't have to do very much to live up to his reputation as a leftish writer of marginally literate Sci-Fi novels with a wayward imagination for extra-terrestial sexuality. His fabricated visions of the future were, so he was told by his students at the interview, *laid back*: a phrase he decided which meant one was resigned, aware, controlled, relaxed and in command without actually striving to be so. In other words he'd been roped in because the students had, endearingly, confused his imaginative fabrications with his personality. It was the sort of confusion Carlo found charming: and *charming* was a word he used with noticeable frequency.

We may consider further details of the picture: again the phraseology is apt for Carlo liked to use the lecturer's lingo to show his views could carry a certain weight:

81

picture him on the way, during an unseasonably cold July, crossing the frontier into Bloomsbury, to the site of a singularly unpleasant murder, a double killing no less which, as the victims would have commented had they achieved resurrection, was the result of a *fantastic situation*.

Details, as Carlo would have said, may be presented by way of preface:

The appointment of Carlo Fortismere, novelist, inspired by the students, confirmed by the college's letter of contract, was greeted with enthusiasm by the institution because the current view was that painting couldn't actually be *taught* in the first place. Drawing was as good as out. Self-expression was a by-word for those inverted outbursts more conveniently confined to the psychiatric clinic. Painting technique you gleaned from a self-directed study of great paintings in London's museums and galleries if you used, and few now seemed to, a brush. Imagination was the thing. This was dragged out in what was called staff-student-one-to-one-confrontation, i.e. *conversation*, which as you can tell by the current substitution of six words for one tended to get a little windy. Carlo's appeal, therefore, lay in his ability for engaging in a kind of relaxed chat about everything under the sun. He was totally relieved to discover the students' delight in him because painting in general wasn't, as the students would have said, his bag. He found the messages of Augustus John quite as banal as those of Jasper John or was he several Johns? 'Yes, of course,' he'd said. 'Jasper Johns – a very plural imagination.' And he soon discovered something he'd have discovered anyway had he thought about it, and he hadn't, namely, that an art student most of all enjoys, and it's perfectly understandable, talking about himself. Or, in this case of murder and for our purposes: herself.

Jane Calderton's paintings reflected herself. The dominant grey matched her eyes. The surrounding edges of black matched her dark hair. The neat shapes she painted might have been derived from her own neat physical proportions. They were the withdrawn, doubting paintings of a withdrawn doubting girl, daughter of a clergyman whose wife had once had a flower piece exhibited by the Royal Academy.

She soon let Carlo know of her interest in his writing. She revealed that she had undertaken a specially careful reading of his novel, *Journey to Solitica 3*. Word for word, she reminded him of *New Society*'s celebration of the Fortismere *approach* based upon '. . . a cogent metaphor for Marxist sexuality.' Never mind that the grammar didn't quite work : Carlo never worried about the meaning of what he assumed to be flattery though he couldn't for the life of him decide quite how one interpreted Marxism between the sheets. 'It's l-l-laid back,' said Jane.

'I'm charmed you approve,' said Carlo.

This encounter took place early in the year but late in the evening, after Carlo had entertained an Australian student with a withering critique of Robert A. Heinlen's books. Cynicism had drained his energy. He was tired now, and ready to leave for the evening at his Battersea flat carrying his briefcase containing the ingredients for a solitary dinner. He was also looking forward to getting mildly drunk. Then Jane detained him. They faced each other in the empty corridor and he sensed that she had already prepared the scheme of their conversation.

'Someone says,' she said, with difficulty, 'that you need to relate bodily experience to the faculty of fantasy.'

Carlo considered this curious declaration. 'Is that what I need?'

'Not specifically,' she told him, giving it thought. Then she laughed. 'Maybe, maybe. If you need to get it together that's a kind of nervous formula. Okay. Let's take it from there sometime.'

Off she clattered, seeming to Carlo very awkward, on her wooden clogs.

It was often the same after that. She lingered, waiting

for him, offered her pearls of wisdom to him and left suddenly. He supposed she had a regular date with someone and began to wonder who. There came a day when she said, 'Carlo, you can't understand the frontier I straddle.'

'I can't?'

'No way,' she said.

'Perhaps you'd allow me to take a closer look at your pictures so I can have a go at understanding it?'

She looked at him angrily. 'You've *already* looked at them.'

He said he had indeed. 'In passing. They're handsome.'

'Wow!' she said. '*Handsome.* I hadn't thought they were *handsome.*' And she looked at him with an intense smile. She was, Carlo thought, a very intense young lady.

'I like it,' she said. 'Handsome . . .'

'Then let's make a time to talk about them.'

'No,' she said, firmly. 'Leave it there. *Handsome.* That's fine. You might spoil it.'

'It's up to you,' he said, and must have looked disappointed because there was consolation in her face.

'You can buy me a coffee,' she said.

'When?'

'Now. I'm not doing anything now.'

'Well,' he said, slightly resentful that she could presume quite so blatantly that he had nothing else to do. 'Perhaps I am doing something.'

'It's your thing,' she said. 'What else are you doing?'

'I'm going home.'

'Okay. Suit yourself.' And off she clattered.

He at once regretted that he had apparently caused her offence. 'All right,' he called after her back view. 'A coffee.'

They went to an Italian place and he bought the coffees. She sat opposite him nervously. Between sips she laughed in a studied sort of way mainly about the other teachers Carlo didn't know. 'They're okay,' she said. 'But if they want to paint then why do they teach dumb-dumbs like me? I mean, like it doesn't add up. You have to make a commitment to painting. It's all or nothing.'

'Is that what you've made?' he asked her.

'Right. To nothing else.'

'To *no one*?'

'There's a guy I like. And you? Is there a woman?'

'I have a wife,' he said.

'What's she like?'

It was a long time since anyone had asked him that. What should he tell her : the truth perhaps?

The truth was that his wife was thirty-three, beautiful, intelligent, a very good lover. Everything, as they say, a man desires; and precisely because she was everything a man desires she had been persuaded by a Swedish furniture designer to join him at his farmhouse. There she embraced the Swede and the life of the self-sufficient; or, as Carlo put it himself, the self-satisfied, the self-opinionated. His wife had simply dedicated herself to three causes : Ecology : Save The Whale and the Re-cycling of Waste Matter. These were causes Carlo recognised as causes he couldn't bring himself to espouse. Thus he made the mistake of ignoring the extent of his wife's concern. He was urban man : she was rural woman. He liked his London messy, seedy, anonymous, marked by men's follies. He thought whales ugly creatures; in fact, he'd never seen one anyway. He thought the proper place for waste matter was down the loo. So when his wife met the Swede, a bearded fellow in brown furs like an autumnal Father Christmas with a bit of the bandit in him too, with a searchlight smile, quoting Lawrence and Joyce from the hip, advocating his personal philosophy of Silence/Exile/Cunning, the electricity was plugged in hard and his wife let herself be taken lights full on.

Carlo was hurt more badly than he could have imagined he would be. Worse still, his wife opted out or, as it were, plugged herself in at the Swedish farm with their two children in tow. Carlo, left alone in Battersea, talked the matter over with a doctor friend who advised him to let her be, let Nature take its course (advice his wife and the confounded Swede would doubtless have applauded from the ecological point of view), let her come to her senses (more applause), to give her the benefit of the doubt. All of which Carlo did more or less. Presumably the Swede and his new someone else's wife interpreted the strategy as apathetic : as a *carte blanche* to pursue a modern liaison to where ever modern liaisons are pursued to. Anyway, she didn't come back, made no demands and Carlo waited it out. So far he'd waited eight months, two weeks and three days. He'd been faithful and very lonely.

So he told Jane a lie :

'My wife's away on holiday with the children. I thought she needed a break from London. You know, domestic drudgery.'

'A heavy situation.'

'Perfectly light-hearted,' said Carlo.

'Do you like my clothes ?' she asked.

'Distinctive,' said Carlo, flashing his reply to the flashed question.

'Is that a put-down ?'

'Do you mean,' he asked her, 'that I'm being critical ?'

She nodded agreement as though expecting to suffer regret.

'Well,' he said, 'I think they're charming.'

Satisfied, she said she had to go. No thanks. No goodbye. Just 'See you around'. Never a single question about himself only the one about his wife. He was left to pick up the bill and to go home again, as usual, alone and melancholy.

Gradually it became a routine. Week after week. He learned she liked J. J. Cale, late Elvis (he was better when he got fat), the films of Fassbinder and the novels of Angela Carter. There was no flirtation, no kiss on the cheek. No touching of any kind at all. No held stares.

Just a lot of talking. All about Jane. She was incredibly interested in herself.

All of which surprised him in a way when the Australian boy called Barney – the one who listened avidly to Carlo's bashing of Heinlen – called him aside one day and said :

'What does Jane mean to you?'

'Charming girl.'

'Yeah, Carlo Fortismere, what else?'

'I don't follow.'

'You have something going?'

'I really don't follow you.'

'Okay, okay . . .' And then, with that stunning respect for tradition that Australians sometimes display he added, 'Like, there's an old college saying about the staff – Don't Handle The Goods.'

'I like mine paper-wrapped,' said Carlo. 'In other words, my friend, it's rude even to sniff at what tempts one in the market place. Mind your bloody manners.'

The Australian's mouth fell open and he looked very angry indeed. So did Jane's when she learned of the encounter. They were on their way to the Italian place.

'What's your flat like?' she asked him.

'Dull. You wouldn't be interested to hear.'

'I would.'

'Really?'

'Really.'

'Would you like to see it?'

'I might. You haven't asked.'

'You wouldn't accept if I did.'

'I might. Try me.'

'Come and have supper.'

It was as sudden as that. A lonely man. The meal cooked by a girl much younger. The gentleness. For the first time all the questions about him. The summer dawn. Cunning love. Our secret. Cleo Laine and John Williams: 'Just close your eyes for that's a lovely way to be . . .

the fundamental loneliness goes whenever two can dream a dream together . . .'

'Why,' he asked her over breakfast, 'was Barney quite so shirty with me?'

'Because,' she said, holding out her fingers and bringing them suddenly to her own heart. 'He's obsessed by me.'

'Are you lovers?'

'We have been.'

'Good heavens.'

'Well, I made him happy . . .'

Just as she's made me happy too, thought Carlo.

'Only,' she said with a smile. 'He's not an adulterer.'

'Thanks a million,' he said. 'I'm only offering a new interpretation for democracy. Shared by consent. Doubtless, the Swedes have a word for it.'

She fell silent and lit a cigarette. 'One thing, Carlo, you'd better leave this to me. He's a violent bloke. He has a record for punch-ups and a stabbing, you know?'

'I didn't. But thanks for telling me. I'll buy a gun.'

'Don't get heavy. He's on pills for it. The whole thing.'

'Let's hope he doesn't forget to take them then.'

Discreetly, they became regular lovers, and the academic year ended with a last telephone call:

'Carlo. This is Jane. Look, there's some trouble. It's Barney.'

He imagined the Australian waving a knife in the air.

'Look. He's been watching your place. He's seen us.'

'What's he going to do about it?'

'He w-wants to s-see you.'

'Very well. I propose we all meet together. A little participatory democracy.'

'Carlo – *please* be serious. Please.' The accent was at its highest nervous upper class.

'I'm being deeply serious,' said Carlo. 'Do remind him, if you would, to take an awful lot of those little pills he takes when he feels a thing coming on.'

'Okay. How many?'

'Really, I've no idea how many. Just a few more, a lot more, than usual. I can't stand violence. I wouldn't know what to do. Especially as he's so keen on one not handling the goods.'

'What?' she asked, unable to understand how this applied to the moment.

'Handling the goods: making love, doing it . . . whatever the latest euphemism is. Oh, don't worry about it. Let's meet in my old office. Violence is less likely to occur on neutral ground. I still have a key – or, if I don't, the porter does.'

All the rest the police discovered when they, in their turn, arrived. After questions, samples of hair, torn clothing, fingerprints, blood tests; after all the complex pattern of forensic investigation; after more questions the last paragraphs emerged.

Very drugged, very drunk, the Australian had used his knife on Jane many times. Then he had turned it on himself, drawing the blade straight across his throat. Mr Carlo Fortismere, the novelist, had arrived, had examined the bodies, had held the head of the dead girl against his chest hoping to find a flicker of life in the bleeding body, then he'd found the knife and the porter had come in.

'I didn't do it,' he said, in shock.

'We know that,' said the policeman with all the authority of the man who has no fear of contradiction.

'I'm sorry,' said Carlo.

'Yes,' said the copper.

'No, I mean I'm sorry,' Carlo said again. 'I'm sorry I got involved.'

'No need to apologise to me, sir, people always are sorry.'

'If only they'd have listened to reason,' offered Carlo.

'Funny name, Fortismere,' said the copper. 'I've read it somewhere . . .'

My God, thought Carlo, I hope he's not a Sci-Fi buff into the bargain.

Fortunately the porter broke in here: 'I'll make you a cup of tea,' he said to Carlo. And then, turning to the policemen, he offered all of them tea too.

By now the senior policeman was getting closer to Carlo's identity as a weaver of extra-terrestial sexual fantasies. But he may have been a compassionate man: a man who recognised that writers like policemen often don't like being reminded of what they do for a living. In any case, he obviously liked an educated turn of phrase for he suddenly said with stern yet colossal jollity: 'We'll all participate in that democratic offer, if we may . . .' The pompous flow dried up on the dot.

The phrases struck a chord in Carlo's memory, artlessness in an artless college of art, and eventually, like the tea itself, the words stuck in his throat.

John Buxton Hilton

SASKJA

It was one of those outer suburbs where you were still aware of the nucleus of the original village : that's if your eye could blot out the multi-storey car park, the Bingo-postered cinema, and the friendly neighbourhood local that looked like an electrical components factory. Disposing of all that gave Kenworthy no difficulty. Although he claimed never to have been here before, he led me unerringly round a dozen right angles to a mews pub called, imponderably, *The Scissors*, where we stood and gazed at an oil painting of the front of the inn that hung in the lounge over a space where at some time or other there had been a fire-place.

'Millard's work?' And the landlord nodded. It was a bad painting, so bad that it was barely credible. 'He's had things hung in the Royal Academy.' But he wouldn't even have thought of submitting this cynical piece. There was no light and shade. It was a square-cut, head-on view with no discernible effort at composition, the detail of every brick shown with impossible precision, as a five-year-old will draw buttons all the way down a man's coat. There was none of the idiosyncrasy generally associated with Millard's work : no chicken's down glued to the ridge-tiles, no deliberate rents in the canvas. He was supposed to have a supreme contempt for the taste of public and critics alike, but it appeared that he had a completely different attitude to the rightness of the customer when he was painting for drinks.

'He comes in here a lot, does he?'

'When he can afford to. And sometimes when he can't.'

'His wife comes with him?'

'It goes in bouts. Sometimes she won't let him out of her sight for weeks at a time.'

Now Millard's current girl-friend was dead, the base of her skull fractured by a short-arm chop with the tool used for lifting the lid of an old iron stove. His wife was being held for protracted interview at the divisional station – and from what we had picked up over the phone, it was only expected to be a matter of the usual patience, boredom and suggestive solicitude before she pro vided the necessary evidence against herself. D.I. Oddy seemed confident that he'd have her singing before we arrived.

Perhaps Kenworthy was content to take his time in *The Scissors* so that Oddy could get well on. But if I'd dared to appear critical, he'd have come out with the familiar rationalisation: time spent sneaking in and out of corners, whilst the local bods thought you were still on your way, was worth its weight in radio-active isotopes.

'Been coming here a long time, has he?'

'I've been here six years, and I reckon I took him over with the fittings.'

'Gets on well with the regulars, does he?'

'You could call him popular. Always ready to do a cartoon for a pint. And there's a game he likes playing with strangers. You make any old smudge on a piece of paper and he turns it into something.'

'Something bloody filthy as a rule, I shouldn't wonder.'

'There was no harm in Jack Millard,' the landlord said, resenting the implication that anything obscene might be appreciated on his premises. I noticed that he'd gone over to the past tense, as if he believed that a phase of Millard's existence was over. 'But it's no use trying to hide the facts: he was moody. He had ideas, but I don't think they could always find their way out. And since he picked this weasel up – '

'Weasel?'

'Nice little thing, it was. Not that it was much use trying to tell that to the ladies. Picked it up on the edge of the Common, he had. Reckoned he'd saved its life.'

'And he used to bring it in here?'

'He never went anywhere without it. He said it thought he was its mother.'

'When did this start?'

'Two or three weeks ago.'

I then caught the look in Kenworthy's eye that said that his interest in what was going on in the divisional station was even less than it had been five minutes ago. He caught the look in mine, too, and sent me off to liaise with the local toilers. I did not hear the full story of Saskja until Kenworthy was ready to conjure a solution out of thin air, but I might as well tell it now as I heard it later.

Millard had caught – in fact, rescued – the animal in a wilderness shrubbery on the edge of an acre of prim-eval Common. Pause for Lounge Bar admiration of the miracles of Outer London ecology. He had snatched her from under the evil green eyes of a cat who had already delivered one playful body-blow. Why she was out of her nest, and what had happened to the rest of the brood, are mysteries that remain on the file. I do not know how difficult it is to determine the sex of a baby weasel, but Millard seemed to harbour no doubts on the point. He explained to the clientele of *The Scissors* that he had named her after Rembrandt's wife. And he took the animal home for the conventional nurture with milk from an eye-dropper and weaning on shreds of raw meat. 'It seems obvious,' Kenworthy said, 'that what got hold of Millard was the emotional state of the animal: her para-lytic fear. And fear remained the hallmark of the creature's existence, except when she was either in direct contact with his body or entangled somewhere amongst his clothes.'

Everywhere that Millard went, Saskja had to go. It

was not a matter into which his personal choice had much chance to enter. A minute or two after his first pint was drawn, the inquisitive snout and whiskers would appear out of his cuff or from under his collar, burrowing in the curls at the back of his neck, nibbling at the lobe of his ear, or emerging from a furrow in his beard. There were some in *The Scissors* who believed that it was his sweater, rather than the man himself, that the animal was really attached to.

The first time the weasel was introduced into the pub, there was general consternation. Her fright at the strange surroundings and even stranger smells sent her scurrying into the darkest and least accessible corner. There was the usual fuss from women who intuitively feared the propensity of small furry mammals to seek dark and intimate refuge. Millard took command of the peak-hour bar with startling aggression : the mild sardonic anarchist turned suddenly sergeant-major.

'Everybody still! Nobody move a foot an inch!'

He told the landlord afterwards that he did not know how Saskja could possibly not be trodden on. The horror of it transfixed him. But on his hands and knees he somehow retrieved her from under the piano. She scuttled up his sleeve and it was at least ten minutes before the tip of her nose appeared under his adam's apple.

'She wants to poop,' Millard explained to the company, claiming that he already had Saskja house-trained, or rather that she had trained herself, for she always performed in the same spot behind the cardboard box in which she was parted from him when he went to bed. And how, *The Scissors* asked Millard's wife, did she react to sharing the marital chamber with a weasel?

They were in the middle of one of those periods, Kenworthy learned, in which not only Saskja, but also Cath Millard went everywhere their master went. Whatever rhyme or reason underlaid Millard's wife's sporadic vigilance, the pattern of it escaped *The Scissors*. She seemed to go through spells of possessiveness during which she

94

was at Millard's elbow if he only went out for cigarettes. Yet there were other occasions when she must have known damned well that he was having a dirty night out, while she sat at home and darned his socks in apparent tranquillity. To Kenworthy it all seemed perfectly simple. 'There were times, Shiner, when she knew she could afford to indulge his passing fancies – and perhaps even save herself the effort and bother of attending to him. But she always had it weighed up to a nicety when it was more than a passing fancy. She knew which rival attractions posed a lasting threat to herself as sitting tenant. And when she saw those danger signs, she moved in.

'By the time we got on to this, Shiner, the lunch-hour trade had started, and I was able to tap quite ⌐ few new seams of opinion. They may be a bit weak in *The Scissors* at drawing philosophical conclusions, but they do have an eye for a fact. And I wouldn't care to be the habitué who wants to hide his amorous twinges from them. They all knew well enough where Millard's eyes were wandering this time. And the funny thing is – at least, they think it's funny in *The Scissors* – he'd known Jenny Hurst for donkey's years without taking a second look at her. Then, all of a sudden, he thinks she's worth painting. And Cath's up the wing on the ball like a good 'un.'

It was for the murder of Jenny Hurst that D.I. Oddy was working up to charge Cath Millard.

'And it isn't only the ins and outs of bed that people know about,' Kenworthy said. 'It's other things, too. Like the way Millard was getting himself tied up with Saskja. *Unhealthy*, I heard someone call it. *Unclean* isn't the word you'd expect them to use in *The Scissors*. And *unnatural* is perhaps a bit abstract for them. But *unhealthy* – that hits it off. It wasn't quite like a medieval warlock with a familiar. It wasn't black magic. It was a personal relationship. Saskja was giving Millard something he hadn't had in his life before. Something he needed. Something you wouldn't lightly deprive him of. Maybe it was the first time he'd ever been a mother.'

'You mean,' I said, 'that this was one of those times where his wife felt the menace?'

'I'm not sure. Once when he'd drunk too much, he started telling the bar how Saskja had nibbled her way out of her box one night and crept into bed with them. And somebody as a joke asked Cath what she thought of that kind of competition. She had the good sense to make a joke out of it herself, which doesn't suggest that she was letting jealousy get out of hand. But she was fed up with it. And it was interesting to learn the weasel's reaction to her. It tolerated her – that was the extent of its affection. It treated her with a sort of undemonstrative courtesy. As the landlord put it : it was as if it wanted to show it knew its manners – no more.'

'But how did this lead to the death of Jenny Hurst?'

'Ah, well, it doesn't go in a straight line. Things seldom do. Bear with me a minute, Shiner. There's more to come. There must be some in *The Scissors* who watch nature programmes on the telly, because they asked Millard what he was going to do when Saskja started responding to the calls of her kind – as she was surely going to within a matter of weeks now. The old hormones would start doing their stuff, the hunting instinct would assert itself, she'd scent a male of the species. Or, more likely, he'd scent her. What was Millard going to do then? Liberate her on the edge of the Common? That was right and proper, wasn't it? Maybe she'd have the good breeding to look in and see him from time to time.

Kenworthy yawned. The case was over and he was physically tired.

Millard's reaction took the pub by surprise.

' "I shall kill her," he said. "She'll go under my heel. It'll be instantaneous."

' "But surely," someone said, "that's not necessary. The survival instinct – "

' "No. She'd be in the claws of an owl in less than ten minutes. There are things I haven't been able to teach

96

her, things she'd have learned from her mother and her siblings."

'The frank callousness of the man – or so it seemed to *The Scissors* – was outside their range of normal conceptions. And Millard had had enough to drink to make him quarrelsome.

' "I shall take her life. But at least I shall spare her terror."

'And he suddenly picked Saskja up and held her in front of his face, so that the pair of them were looking into each other's eyes.

' "Because she's beautiful. That's what she is. And she needs me."

'Uninhibited emotion embarrassed them, as it always does in places like *The Scissors*, except when it's merely aggressive. It also embarrassed Millard's wife, who started muttering that he was giving people a totally wrong impression of himself – to which, I fear, he responded with bad grace. Then Jenny Hurst came in and wanted to see Saskja and handle her, which Millard would not allow because, he said, the strange touch and smell would drive the creature out of its mind. The Millards left very shortly after that, at Cath's insistence. Jenny Hurst was a deviation that she did not permit – even when she was being held at arm's distance from a weasel. And Millard must have been pretty astute at picking up the danger signs. He followed his wife meekly into the night.

'A peculiar set-up,' Kenworthy said. 'And I think things were waiting to be brought to a head before Saskja came on the scene. But it was Saskja who ushered in the grand finale.'

That was the state of information and opinion that Kenworthy had reached by the time that he joined D.I. Oddy and me in a semi-circle round Cath Millard. But I, of course, knew nothing of it, beyond the fact that Millard had recently made a pet of a weasel; and D.I. Oddy did not even know that.

He was not pleased to see me. He was not pleased to

have Kenworthy exercising oversight in his division, even less to have a sergeant moving in as advance-guard. Bert Oddy was an easy man to displease – especially when he had decided that displeasure was to be his image for the day. And Cath Millard was doing nothing to brighten his vision of life. She wasn't prepared to admit that he had her cold.

He had – or thought he had, I had yet to see the case-notes – circumstantial evidence to his own satisfaction. He had not so far revealed any of it to her, but would be doing so grudgingly, an item at a time, in the hope of persuading her how foolish and wayward she was being, not to complete the story for him. His method – I suppose he had at least started with an appeal to reason – had reached the bullying stage. And it was producing no effect on her at all.

She was a plain woman, additionally unattractive perhaps because of the way in which they had hurried her from home with minimal opportunity to think of appearances; no accident, that, of course. It was difficult to know whether she ever had been anything to look at. She was sharp-featured, and her cheek-bones could have betokened hunger, austerity – or years of progress towards reluctantly admitting non-fulfilment. She was in her mid-thirties; perhaps seven or eight years younger than Millard. A thinking woman, I could not help believing, as I sat in on Oddy's interrogation, whether an innocent one or not. Her entire effort was concentrated on producing a serenity that was pushing Oddy to exasperation. He could not shake her story, and she was determined that he should not rattle her composure. Not once did she raise her voice. Never did she attempt to underline a plain statement with artificial emphasis.

I was asked in to take notes, ostensibly to release Oddy's sergeant for an existing surfeit of divisional chores. It may also have been lip-service to the imminence of Kenworthy. One could never be certain of anything, with Oddy.

'We'll run over it again, for Sergeant Wright's benefit, shall we, Mrs Millard? Shall we tell him step by step how we passed yesterday evening? At what time did your husband go out to his studio?'

'It is you who told me he went to his studio. I did not know that at the time. He told me, and I believed him, that he was going to collect some old picture-frames from Arthur Guppy.'

'Which you knew he would be taking to the studio.'

'I did not think about it. I assumed he would bring them back here first.'

'Yet you admitted just now that that would have meant a double journey with an awkward load.'

'I did not think about it.'

'You knew that he was taking a suspicious interest in a divorced woman called Jenny Hurst.'

'I did know that.'

'And it was causing you considerable concern.'

'I was doing my best to discourage it.'

'How?'

'By denying him as far as I could the opportunity to be in her company.'

'Yet last night you presented him with sudden freedom.'

'It did not occur to me that his errand might not be genuine. He could have been back in the house in twenty minutes, and he knew that supper was nearly ready.'

'A hot meal, or cold?'

'Veal and ham pie and salad.'

'Nothing that needed watching whilst you followed him down to the studio yourself.'

'I did not go to the studio.'

'We have picked up one of your gloves on the cobbles outside.'

'That defeats my understanding.'

'And there was fresh size in the welts of your outdoor shoes.'

'There often is.'

'*Fresh* size, Mrs Millard. When do you claim you were last in the studio?'

'Three days ago. Monday afternoon. That is not a claim. It is a fact.'

Oddy weighed up his tactics. Doubtless he had other circumstantial bombshells in reserve. If so, he decided to save them.

'You have been worried by your husband's interest in Jenny Hurst?'

'Very.'

'Why, in particular? It's not unknown for you to give him a fair ration of slack, is it?'

'I know I can usually rely on him to tire of anyone bar me in less than a week. But I thought Jenny Hurst might have longer term plans for him.'

'It's very helpful to declare your own motive for murder.'

'I am merely trying to convince you of my good faith.'

'There's only one thing that I'm convinced of, as far as you're concerned,' Oddy said. And so it went on : Oddy hectoring and repetitious, Mrs Millard provocatively reasonable, a war of attrition in which the aggressor was pathetically oblivious of his victim's reserves. After another three quarters of an hour of it, Kenworthy breezed in, a winnowing wind. I knew, of course, that for some time now he had been looking for a chance to move in on one of Oddy's cases. He put on his swash-buckling act in the process of opening the door, and was firing staccato questions before he had closed it behind him.

'Where've you put Millard?'

'Cooling his heels in another room.'

'Have him fetched. We'll all go down to the scene of the crime. What's *she* got to say for herself?'

He glanced casually over Cath Millard, who straightened herself in her chair. When Kenworthy was fanning with fans, there was seldom much idle chaff about.

'Being stupid,' Oddy said. Kenworthy looked at her

for a silent second, then asked her a single question, in a tone of a relative enquiring about a mutual friend.

'Where's Saskja?'

'Saskja?'

'When did you last see your weasel?'

We could see that the question reminded her of something forgotten.

'Come to think of it, I haven't seen her since – '

'Since?'

'Since my husband left the house yesterday evening to collect some picture-frames.'

Oddy made impatient noises which Kenworthy did not seem to hear. He told me afterwards how much he was relying on her reaction. There was a great deal that he needed to know about her, and he got to know much of it in a moment of time. He saw at once that the question disturbed her, but she was not shaken by it. Her answer was quick enough to be truthful. And he believed that in that instant she came to the same conclusion as he had.

'Let's have a quick note of the timings,' he said to Oddy, and that proved untidy, because Oddy had got his theories inextricably mixed up with the facts.

8.30, Millard left house, ostensibly to fetch frames. Expected home from nine o'clock onwards, but in effect had already admitted an appointment with Mrs Jenny Hurst, who met him in the *Green Man* at 8.45, and went with him to the studio about ten minutes later. He claimed that his wife burst in on them in a blazing rage and had a row with Jenny Hurst in which insults were exchanged until they came to blows. Cath Millard struck the woman at the back of the head with an iron implement. The timing was consonant with the pathologist's provisional brackets for death. According to Millard, his wife then stormed out. He himself did not report the incident at the police station until 1.30 a.m. having, he stated, spent the intervening time wandering about the streets and Common in shock and distress, unable to apply his mind to what had happened. A glove belonging to Mrs Millard had been found in the lane outside the studio, and her outdoor shoes had been found to bear traces of fresh size.

'To the studio, then.'

It lay between the last row of shops and the edge of a strip of urban heath. It was a ramshackle, pre-first-war building that had once been a cabinet maker's workshop. The woodwork and paint were in poor condition and a patch of ground round three of its sides was uncultivated. Inside, the air was heavy with turpentine, damp rot and congealed blood, but there was evidence of plenty of unfinished work. Pictures were stacked and leaning against the walls, sick caprices, most of them. Millard specialised in whimsical iconoclasm. He knew what social institutions he would like to see destroyed, but appeared to have nothing to put in their place. His human figures were uncharitably ugly and complacently stupid: the Sunday afternoon parade in a provincial cemetery; American tourists photographing a Palace guard on crutches.

But our attention was immediately claimed by the arrangement in the middle of the room – a double divan, now stripped down to a blood-sodden mattress that looked, against the dust and greyness, almost as if it were part of a film-set, except that in place of a camera there stood an easel, with the charcoal outline of a reclining woman on primed hardboard. Kenworthy's eyes went quickly round for obvious evidence, but everything of vital interest had already gone to Forensic; there was no faulting Oddy over technical routines. Kenworthy now faced Millard and asked him in quiet, one might almost say sympathetic tones, 'Where's Saskja?'

Millard's reaction was different from what his wife's had been. To him the question did come as a shock. He closed his eyes and rocked back on his heels, so that I stood by for him to faint. But he quickly recovered, shifted his stance, and looked at us with unconvincing incomprehension.

'Saskja?'

There was a crack in his voice, but I felt sceptical about it.

'I'm only too sorry I can't show her to you.'

'Why can't you?'

'Do you mind if I sit down?'

Kenworthy motioned him to a broken-backed Windsor chair.

'There was an affray here last night. That's why you're here, isn't it? And Saskja was the first casualty.'

'How? And by whom?'

'Trodden underfoot. Scared out of her wits.'

'And what have you done with her?'

'Buried her.'

'When did you have time to do that?'

'Last night.'

'Where?'

Millard's eyes slowly flickered: a pause, whilst he gathered resolution.

'I don't propose to answer that. You're not going to – '

'I'm going to do whatever comes into my head. Sergeant Wright – '

He told me to take a constable and search the immediate surrounds.

'And you know what you're looking for?'

'Freshly turned earth, sir. Disturbance to vegetation. Soil surplus from filling in.'

Ironically, it sounded like a check-list from the *Police Promotion Handbook*. The constable would not believe that what we were looking for was a mounded patch some eight inches by three. Millard had even arranged a few petals in a vase made from the screw-cap of a paint-tube. We scrabbled out earth, and about six inches down our finger-nails scraped the lid of a coffin. This was what Millard had been making when he said he was walking the streets. He had done a neat little job, whilst his short-term mistress had been lying on a brain-soaked pillow only a foot or two away from the bench where he was working. We carried the coffin indoors, and Millard rose in protest.

'I take the strongest possible exception – '

'The National Council for Civil Liberties hasn't got round to weasels yet, Millard.'

And Kenworthy looked round for something with which to prise open the lid. Fortunately one of our constables was close to Millard's elbow, and quick to restrain him. He had spent two midnight hours alone with the woman's corpse; but he could not bear to see Saskja again.

The wood split, and Kenworthy levered up the lid. He brought out the carcase with what I can only describe as gentle respect. And equally tenderly he felt at the dead flesh with his finger-tips.

'I don't believe that this animal was trodden underfoot.'

'*She* killed her,' Millard said.

But of course Kenworthy insisted on a post mortem. I shall always believe that this was partly for the grotesque joy of laying Saskja on the slab, and then calling the pathologist to tell him that he had another one for him.

The pathologist was a devoted man, with all that puerile insistence on the macabre that is often such men's defence against their calling. He kept us waiting for his report on Jenny Hurst, and when it came it was full of those painstaking irrelevancies which turned her pathetically from a corpse back into a woman. She had died from a blow with an unresilient object, and blood and hair found on the handle from the stove-lid was consonant with its having been the weapon used. There was an aroma of gin in her stomach, and the partially digested remains of about half a packet of potato crisps.

'Plain? Or salt and vinegar?' Kenworthy asked.

Then he broke the news that another specimen was waiting in Laboratory B. I stood by whilst the pair of them mounted a minute or two of their characteristic cross-talk.

The pathologist let us watch him work. He applied the scalpel lovingly, and peeled back Saskja's fur with delicacy.

'We might cut a few corners if you tell me in advance what we're looking for.'

'Traces of nail-varnish under the skin at the nape of the neck. And if we could identify the brand, it would help.'

We showed Millard the full typed report: not only acetone under the skin, but even the approximate timing of Saskja's last meal: roughly 3 cc of uncooked beefburger. I think it was the cold precision of that that broke him. He told us how he had barely begun to make love to Jenny when Saskja, having gnawed her way out of the carton in which he had exiled her on his bench, suddenly darted up the mattress and began to wriggle down between their bodies. Jenny lost her head. She seized the animal and tried to choke it to death, and when she found that this needed more strength than she had in her fingers, she swung it by its hindquarters and beat its head against the wall. That was when Millard had gone for the stove-handle.

In our last session with him he seemed obsessively, one might almost say recklessly honest. He was a strange man: very talented, Kenworthy and I were inclined to think. Yet he lacked something: application, discipline, whatever. Hence his tendency to blame society for not appreciating him. He had been sketching in his remand cell: a painfully living pencil study of Saskja cowering before advancing talons. Human talons.

'I'll tell you what,' he said. 'I learned more from Saskja than I ever did from any woman. But then, Saskja was a woman, too, wasn't she? I read a story once where a man had just murdered his lady-friend, and he seized her by the shoulders, and screamed that he was sorry, and called to her to come back. But not me. For me it was the most natural thing in the world to get quietly on with making that coffin, whilst Jenny lay in a twisted heap. Saskja was worth five of her. There ought to be something in the laws of the land to compel every couple to keep a weasel for a week or two. It would be surprising what truths would out.'

What struck me while he was talking was Kenworthy's grave attention to every word he said. There was nothing in Millard's views that seemed to strike Kenworthy as even slightly off-beam.

'And it came to me, while I was sand-papering a panel, what a relief it would be to Cath, too, to know that Saskja had gone. "It's got to be her or me," she'd said to me earlier that day, meaning Jenny. And at that very moment Saskja's snout peeped out from my cuff, and I saw Cath's eyes light on her. There were some things that even Cath wouldn't put into words. But then she didn't need to. Cath didn't nag me – often. She had the knack of getting her own way by simply being there.

'That was when it came to me that now was the time to organise myself a clean sheet. Short interval for cynical laughter : no more weasels in bed, clean sheet. So I dropped one of Cath's gloves, doctored the welt of her shoe. I was going to set myself free : as free as an over-protected weasel turned back on the heath.

'So am I sorry about all that has happened? Well, yes, I am. I'm going to be imprisoned for life, and that gives a man something to be sorry for. But not for them. Not for the women. Not even for Saskja. She was going to be the biggest tyrant of the three. I can see that now.'

And he made a dive for his pencil sketch, screwed it up into a ball and flung it against the wall of his cell.

Peter Lovesey

THE LOCKED ROOM

Sometimes when the shop was quiet Braid would look up at the ceiling and give a thought to the locked room overhead. He was mildly curious, no more. If the police had not taken an interest he would never have done anything about it.

The inspector appeared one Wednesday soon after eleven, stepping in from Leadenhall Street with enough confidence about him to show he was no tourist. Neither was he in business; it is one of the City's most solemn conventions that between ten and four nobody is seen on the streets in a coat. This was a brown imitation leather coat, categorically not City at any hour. Gaunt and pale, a band of black hair trained across his head to combat baldness, he stood back from the counter, not interested in buying cigarettes, waiting rather, one hand in a pocket of the coat, the other fingering his woollen tie, while the last genuine customer named his brand and took his change.

When the door was shut he came a step closer and told Braid, 'I won't take up much of your time. Detective Inspector Gent, C.I.D.' The hand that had been in the pocket now exhibited a card. 'Routine inquiry. You are Frank Russell Braid, the proprietor of this shop?'

Braid nodded, and moistened his lips. He was perturbed at hearing his name articulated in full like that, as if he were in court. He had never been in trouble with the police. Never done a thing he was ashamed of. Twenty-seven years he had served the public loyally over this counter. He had not received a single complaint he could recollect, nor made one. From the small turnover he achieved he had always paid whatever taxes the government imposed. Some of his customers – bankers, brokers and accountants – made fortunes and talked openly of tax dodges. That was not Frank Braid's way. He believed in fate. If it was decreed that he should one day be rich, it would happen. Meanwhile he would continue to retail cigarettes and tobacco honestly and without regret.

'I believe you also own the rooms upstairs, sir?'

'Yes.'

'There is a tenant, I understand.'

So Messiter had been up to something. Braid clicked his tongue, thankful that the suspicion was not directed his way, yet irritated at being taken in. From the beginning Messiter had made a good impression. The year of his tenancy had seemed to confirm it. An educated man, decently dressed, interesting to talk to and completely reliable with the rent. This was a kick in the teeth.

'His name, sir?'

'Messiter.' With deliberation Braid added, 'Norman Henry Messiter.'

'How long has Mr Messiter been a lodger here?'

'*Lodger* isn't the word. He uses the rooms as a business address. He lives in Putney. He started paying rent in September last year. That would be thirteen months, wouldn't it?'

It was obvious from the inspector's face that this was familiar information. 'Is he upstairs this morning, sir?'

'No. I don't see a lot of Mr Messiter. He calls on Tuesdays and Fridays to collect the mail.'

'Business correspondence?'

'I expect so. I don't examine it.'

'But you know what line Mr Messiter is in?'

It might have been drugs from the way the inspector put the question.

'He deals in postage stamps.'

'It's a stamp shop upstairs?'

'No. It's all done by correspondence. This is simply the address he uses when he writes to other dealers.'

'Odd,' the inspector commented. 'I mean, going to the expense of renting rooms when he could just as easily carry on the business from home.'

Braid would not be drawn. He would answer legitimate questions, but he was not going to volunteer opinions. He busied himself tearing open a carton of cigarettes.

'So it's purely for business?' the inspector resumed. 'Nothing happens up there?'

That started Braid's mind racing. Nothing *happens* .. ? What did they suspect? Orgies? Blue films?

'It's an unfurnished flat,' he said. 'Kitchen, bathroom and living room. It isn't used.'

At that the inspector rubbed his hands. 'Good. In that case you can show me over the place without intruding on anyone's privacy.'

It meant closing for a while, but most of his morning regulars had been in by then.

'Thirteen months ago you first met Mr Messiter,' the inspector remarked on the stairs.

Strictly it was untrue. As it was not put as a question, Braid made no response.

'Handsome set of banisters, these, Mr Braid. Individually carved, are they?'

'The building is at least two hundred years old,' Braid told him, grateful for the distraction. 'You wouldn't think so to look at it from Leadenhall Street. You see, the front has been modernised. I wouldn't mind an old-fashioned front if I were selling silk hats or umbrellas, but cigarettes – '

'Need a more contemporary display,' the inspector cut in as if he had heard enough. '*Was* it thirteen months ago you first met Mr Messiter?'

Clearly this had some bearing on the police enquiry. It was no use prevaricating. 'In point of fact, no. More like two years.' As the inspector's eyebrows peaked in interest,

Braid launched into a rapid explanation. 'It was purely in connection with the flat. He came in here one day and asked if it was available. Just like that, without even seeing over the place. At the time, I had a young French couple as tenants. I liked them and I had no intention of asking them to leave. Besides, I know the law. You can't do that sort of thing. I told Mr Messiter. He said he liked the situation so much that he would wait till they moved out, and to show good faith he was ready to pay the first month's rent as a deposit.'

'Without even seeing inside?'

'It must seem difficult to credit, but that was how it was,' said Braid. 'I didn't take the deposit, of course. Candidly, I didn't expect to see him again. In my line of business you sometimes get people coming in off the street simply to make mischief. Well, the upshot was that he *did* come back – repeatedly. I must have seen the fellow once a fortnight for the next eleven months. I won't say I understood him any better, but at least I knew he was serious. So when the French people eventually went back to Marseilles Mr Messiter took over the flat.' By now they were standing on the bare boards of the landing. 'The accommodation is unfurnished,' he said in explanation. 'I don't know what you hope to find.'

If Inspector Gent knew, he was not saying. He glanced through the open door of the bathroom. The place had the smell of disuse.

He reverted to his theme. 'Strange behaviour, waiting all that time for a flat he doesn't use.' He stepped into the kitchen and tried a tap. Water the colour of weak tea spattered out. 'No furniture about,' he went on. 'You must have thought it was odd, not bringing furniture.'

Braid passed no comment. He was waiting by the door of the locked room. This, he knew, was where the interrogation would begin in earnest.

'What's this – the living room?' the inspector asked. He came to Braid's side and tried the door. 'Locked. May I have the key, Mr Braid?'

'That isn't possible, I'm afraid. Mr Messiter changed the lock. We – er – came to an agreement.'

The inspector seemed unsurprised. 'Paid some more on the rent, did he? I wonder why.' He knelt by the door. 'Strong lock. Chubb mortice. No good trying to open that with a piece of wire. How did he justify it, Mr Braid?'

'He said it was for security.'

'It's secure, all right.' Casually, the inspector asked, 'When did you last see Mr Messiter?'

'Tuesday.' Braid's stomach lurched. 'You don't suspect he is – '

'Dead in there? No, sir. Messiter is alive, no doubt of that. Active, I would say.' He grinned in a way Braid found disturbing. 'But I wouldn't care to force this without a warrant. I'll be arranging that. I'll be back.' He started downstairs.

'Wait,' said Braid, going after him. 'As the landlord, I think I have the right to know what you suspect is locked in that room.'

'Nothing dangerous or detrimental to health, sir,' the inspector told him without turning his head. 'That's all you need to know. You trusted Messiter enough to let him fit his own lock, so with respect you're in no position to complain about rights.'

After the inspector had left, Braid was glad he had not been stung into a response he regretted, but he was angry, and his anger refused to be subdued through the rest of the morning and afternoon. It veered between the inspector, Messiter and himself. He recognised now his mistake in agreeing to the fitting of the lock, but to be rebuked like a gullible idiot was unjust. Messiter's request had seemed innocent enough at the time. Well, it had crossed Braid's mind that what was planned could be the occasional afternoon up there with a girl, but he had no objection to that if it was discreet. He was not narrow-minded. In its two centuries of existence the room must have seen some passion. Crime was quite another thing, not to be countenanced.

He had trusted Messiter, been impressed by his sincerity. The man had seemed genuinely enthusiastic about the flat, its old-world charm, the high, corniced ceilings and the solid doors. To wait, as he had, over a year for the French people to leave had seemed a commitment, an assurance of good faith.

It was mean and despicable. Whatever was locked in that room had attracted the interest of the police. Messiter must have known this was a possibility when he took the rooms. He had cynically and deliberately put at risk the reputation of the shop. Customers were quick to pick up the taint of scandal. When this got into the papers years of goodwill and painstaking service would go for nothing.

That afternoon when Braid's eyes turned to the ceiling, he was not merely curious about the locked room. He was asking questions. Angry, urgent questions.

By six, when he closed, the thing had taken a grip on his mind. He had persuaded himself he had a right to know the extent of Messiter's deceit. Dammit, the room belonged to him. He would not sleep without knowing what was behind that locked door.

And he had thought of a way of doing it.

In the back was a wooden ladder some nine feet long. Years before, when the shop was a glover's, it had been used to reach the high shelves behind the counter. Modern shop design kept everything in easy reach. Where gloves had once been stacked in white boxes were displays of Marlboro country and the pure gold of Benson and Hedges. One morning in the summer he had taken the ladder outside the shop to investigate the working of the sun-blind, which was jammed. Standing several rungs from the top he had been able to touch the ledge below the window of the locked room.

The evening exodus was over, consigning Leadenhall Street to surrealistic silence, when Braid propped the ladder against the shop-front. The black marble and dark-tinted glass of banks and insurance blocks glinted funereally in the street-lights, only the brighter windows of the Bull's Head at the Aldgate end indicating that life was there, as he began to climb. If anyone chanced to pass that way and challenge him, he told himself, he would inform them with justification that the premises were his own and he was simply having trouble with a lock.

He stepped on to the ledge and drew himself level with the window, which was of the sash type. By using a screwdriver from his pocket he succeeded in slipping aside the iron catch. The lower section was difficult to move, but once he had got it started it slid easily upwards. He climbed inside and took out a torch.

The room was empty.

Literally empty. No furniture, curtains, carpet. Bare floorboards, ceiling and walls, with paper peeled away in several places.

Uncomprehending, he shone the torch over the floorboards. They had not been disturbed in months. He examined the skirting-board, the plaster cornice and the window sill. He could not see how anything could be secreted here. The police were probably mistaken about Messiter. And so was he. With a sense of shame he climbed out of the window and drew it down.

On Friday Messiter came in about eleven as usual, relaxed, indistinguishable in dress from the stockbrokers and bankers : dark suit, old boys' tie, shoes gleaming. With a smile he peeled a note from his wallet and bought his box of five Imperial Panatellas, a ritual that from the beginning had signalled goodwill towards his landlord. Braid sometimes wondered if he actually smoked them. He did not carry conviction as a smoker of cigars. He was a quiet man, functioning best in private conversations. Forty-seven by his own admission, he looked ten years younger, dark-haired with brown eyes that moistened when he spoke of things that moved him.

'Any letters for me, Mr Braid?'

'Five or six.' Braid took them from the shelf behind him. 'How is business?'

'No reason to complain,' Messiter said, smiling. 'My work is my hobby, and there aren't many lucky enough to say that. And how is the world of tobacco? Don't tell me. You'll always do a good trade here, Mr Braid. All the pressures – you can see it in their faces. They need the weed and always will.' Mildly he enquired, 'Nobody called this week asking for me, I suppose?'

Braid had not intended saying anything, but Messiter's manner disarmed him. That and the shame he felt at the suspicions he had harboured impelled him to say, 'Actually there *was* a caller. I had a detective in here – when was it? – Wednesday – asking about you. It was obviously a ridiculous mistake.' He described Inspector Gent's visit without mentioning his own investigation afterwards with the ladder. 'Makes you wonder what the police are up to these days,' he concluded. 'I believe we're all on the computer at Scotland Yard now. This sort of thing is bound to happen.'

'You trust me, Mr Braid. I appreciate that,' Messiter said, his eyes starting to glisten. 'You took me on trust from the beginning.'

'I'm sure you aren't stacking stolen goods upstairs, if that's what you mean,' Braid told him in sincerity.

'But the inspector was not so sure?'

'He said something about a search warrant. Probably by now he has realised his mistake. I don't expect to see him again.'

'I wonder what brought him here,' Messiter said, almost to himself.

'I wouldn't bother about it. It's a computer error.'

'I don't believe so. What did he say about the lock I fitted on the door, Mr Braid?'

'Oh, at the time he seemed to think it was quite sinister.' He grinned. 'Don't worry – it doesn't bother me at all. You consulted me about the damned thing and you pay a pound extra a week for it, so who am I to complain? What you keep in there – if anything – is your business.' He chuckled in a way intended to reassure.

'That detective carried on as if you had a fortune hidden away in there.'

'Oh, but I have.'

Braid felt a pulse throb in his temple.

'It's high time I told you,' said Messiter serenely. 'I suppose I should apologise for not saying anything before. Not that there's anything criminal, believe me. Actually it's a rather remarkable story. I'm a philatelist, as you know. People smile at that and I don't blame them. Whatever name you give it, stamp collecting is a hobby for kids. In the business, we're a little sensitive on the matter. We dignify it with its own technology – dies and watermarks and so forth – but I've always suspected this is partly to convince ourselves that the whole thing is serious and important. Well, it occurred to me four or five years ago that there was a marvellous way of justifying stamp collecting to myself and that was by writing a book about stamps. You must have heard of Rowland Hill, the fellow who started the whole thing off?'

'The Penny Post?'

Messiter nodded. '1840 – the world's first postage stamps, the Penny Black and the Twopence Blue. My idea was not to write a biography of Hill – that's been done several times over by cleverer writers than I – but to analyse the way his idea caught on. The response of the Victorian public was absolutely phenomenal, you know. It's all in the newspapers of the period. I went to the Newspaper Library at Colindale to do my research. I spent weeks over it.' His voice conveyed not fatigue at the memory, but excitement. 'There was so much to read. Reports of Parliament. Letters to the Editor. Special articles describing the collection and delivery of the mail.' He paused, pointing a finger at Braid. 'You're wondering what this has to do with the room upstairs. I'll tell you. Whether it was providence or pure good luck I wouldn't care to say, but one afternoon in that Newspaper Library I turned up *The Times* for a day in May, 1841, and my eye was caught – riveted, I should say – by an announce-

ment in the Personal Column on the front page.'
Messiter's hand went to his pocket and withdrew his
wallet. From it he took a folded piece of paper. 'This is
what I saw.'

Braid took it from him, a photocopy of what was un-
questionably a column of old newspaper type. The significant words had been scored round in ballpoint.

*A Young Lady, being desirous of covering her dressing-
room with cancelled postage stamps, has been so far
encouraged in her wish by private friends as to have
succeeded in collecting 16,000. These, however being
insufficient, she will be greatly obliged if any good-
natured person who may have these otherwise worthless
little articles at their disposal, would assist her in her
whimsical project. Address to Miss E.D., Mr Butt's,
Glover, Leadenhall Street.*

Braid made the connection instantly. His throat went
dry. He read it again. And again.

'You understand?' said Messiter. 'It's a stamp man's
dream – a room literally papered with Penny Blacks!'

'But this was – '

'1841. Right. More than a century ago. Have you
ever looked through a really old newspaper? It's quite
astonishing how easy it is to get caught up in the imme-
diacy of the events. When I read that announcement, I
could see that dressing-room vividly in my imagination:
chintz curtains, gas-brackets, brass bedstead, washstand
and mirror. I could see Miss E.D. with her paste-pot and
brush assiduously covering the wall with stamps. It was
such an exciting idea that it came as a jolt to realise that
it all had happened so long ago that Miss E.D. must
have died about the turn of the century. And what of her
dressing-room? That, surely, must have gone, if not in
the Blitz, then in the wholesale rebuilding of the City.
My impression of Leadenhall Street was that the banks
and insurance companies had lined it from end to end
with gleaming office buildings five storeys high. Even if by
some miracle the shop that had been Butt's the Glover's

had survived, and Miss E.D.'s room *had* been over the shop, common sense told me that those stamps must long since have been stripped from the walls.' He paused, smiled and lighted a cigar.

Braid waited, his heart pounding.

'Yet there was a possibility, remote, but tantalising and irresistible, that someone years ago redecorated the room by papering over the stamps. Any decorator will tell you they sometimes find layer upon layer of wallpaper. Imagine peeling back the layers to find thousands of Penny Blacks and Twopence Blues unknown to the world of philately! These days the commonest are catalogued at ten pounds or so, but find some rarities – inverted watermarks, special cancellations – and you could be up to five hundred a stamp. Maybe a thousand. Mr Braid, I don't exaggerate when I tell you the value of such a room could run to half a million pounds. Half a million for what that young lady in her innocence called worthless little articles!'

Braid had a momentary picture of her upstairs in her crinoline arranging the stamps on the wall. His wall!

As if he read the thought, Messiter said, 'It was my discovery. I went to a lot of trouble. Eventually I found the *Post Office Directory* for 1845 in the British Library. The list of residents in Leadenhall Street included a glover by the name of Butt.'

'So you got the number of this shop?'

Messiter nodded.

'And when you came to Leadenhall Street, here it was, practically the last pre-Victorian building this side of Lloyd's?'

Messiter drew on his cigar, scrutinising Braid.

'All those stamps,' Braid whispered. 'Twenty-seven years I've owned this shop and the flat without knowing that in the room upstairs was a fortune. It took you to tell me that.'

'Don't get the idea it was easy for me,' Messiter pointed out. 'Remember I waited practically a year for those French people to move out. That was a test of character, believe me, not knowing what I would find when I took possession.'

Strangely, Braid felt less resentment towards Messiter than the young Victorian woman who had lived in this building, *his* building, and devised a pastime so sensational in its consequence that his own walls mocked him.

Messiter leaned companionably across the counter. 'Don't look so shattered, chum. I'm not the rat you take me for. Why do you think I'm telling you this?'

Braid shrugged. 'I really couldn't say.'

'Think about it. As your tenant, I did nothing underhand. When I took the flat, didn't I raise the matter of redecoration? You said I was free to go ahead whenever I wished. I admit you didn't know then that the walls were covered in Penny Blacks, but I wasn't certain myself till I peeled back the old layers of paper. What a moment that was!' He paused, savouring the recollection. 'I've had a great year thanks to those stamps. In fact, I've set myself up for some time to come. Best of all, I had the unique experience of finding that room.' He flicked ash from the cigar. 'I estimate there are still upwards of twenty thousand stamps up there, Mr Braid. In all justice, they belong to you.'

Braid stared in amazement.

'I'm serious,' Messiter went on. 'I've made enough to buy a place in the country and write my book. The research is finished. That's been my plan for years, to earn some time, and I've done it. I want no more.'

Frowning, Braid said, 'I don't understand why you're doing this. Is it because of the police? You said there was nothing dishonest.'

'And I meant it, but you are right, Mr Braid. I am a little shaken to hear of your visit from the inspector.'

'What do you mean?'

Messiter asked obliquely, 'When you read your newspaper, do you ever bother with the financial pages?'

Braid gave him a long look. Messiter held his stare.

'If it really has any bearing on this, the answer is no. I don't have much interest in the stock market. Nor any capital to invest,' he added.

'Just as well in these uncertain times,' Messiter commented. 'Blue chip investments have been hard to find these last few years. That's why people have been putting their money into other things. Art, for instance. A fine work of art holds its value in real terms even in a fluctuating economy. So do jewellery and antiques. And stamps, Mr Braid. Lately a lot of money has been invested in stamps.'

'That I can understand.'

'Then you must also understand that information such as this' – he put his hand on the photostat between them – 'is capable of causing flutters of alarm. Over the last year or so I have sold to dealers a number of early English stamps unknown to the market. These people are not fools. Before they buy a valuable stamp, they like to know the history of its ownership. I have had to tell them my story and show them the announcement in *The Times*. That's all right. Generally they need no more convincing. But do you understand the difficulty? It's the prospect of twenty thousand Penny Blacks and Twopence Blues unknown to the stamp world shortly coming on to the market. Can you imagine the effect?'

'I suppose it will reduce the value of stamps people already own.'

'Precisely. The rarities may not be so rare. Rumours begin, and it isn't long before there is a panic and prices tumble.'

'Which is when the sharks move in,' said Braid. 'I see it now. The police probably suspect the whole thing is a fraud.'

Messiter gave a nod.

'But you and I know it isn't a fraud,' Braid went on. 'We can show them the room. I still don't understand why you are giving it up.'

'I told you the reason. I always planned to write my book. And there is something else. It's right to warn you that there is sure to be publicity over this. Newspapers, television – this is the kind of story they relish, the unknown Victorian girl, the stamps undiscovered for over a century. Mr Braid, I value my privacy. I don't care for my name being printed in the newspapers. It will happen, I'm sure, but I don't intend to be around when it does. That's why I am telling nobody where I am going. After the whole thing has blown over, I'll send you a forwarding address, if you would be so kind . . .'

'Of course, but – '

A customer came in, one of the regulars. Braid gave him a nod and wished he had gone to the kiosk up the street.

Messiter picked up the conversation. 'Was it a month's notice we agreed? I'll see that my bank settles the rent.' He took the keys of the flat from his pocket and put them on the counter with the photostat. 'For you. I shan't need these again.' Putting a hand on Braid's arm, he added, 'Some time we must meet and have a drink to Miss E.D.'s memory.'

He turned and left the shop and the customer asked for twenty Rothmans. Braid lifted his hand in a belated salute through the shop window and returned to his business. More customers came in. Fridays were always busy with people collecting their cigarettes for the weekend. He was thankful for the activity. It compelled him to adjust by degrees and accept that he was a rich man now. Unlike Messiter, he would not object to the story getting into the press. Some of these customers who had used the shop for years and scarcely acknowledged him as a human being would choke on their toast and marmalade when they saw his name one morning in *The Times*.

It satisfied him most to recover what he owned. When Messiter had disclosed the secret of the building, it was as if the twenty-seven years of Braid's tenure were obliterated. The place was full of Miss E.D. That young lady

– she would always be young – had in effect asserted her prior claim. He had doubted if he would ever again believe it was truly his own. But now that her 'whimsical project' had been ceded to him, he was going to take pleasure in dismantling the design, stamp by stamp, steadily accumulating a fortune Miss E.D. had never supposed would accrue. Vengeful it might be, but it would exorcise her from the building that belonged to him.

Ten minutes before closing time Inspector Gent entered the shop. As before, he waited for the last customer to leave.

'Sorry to disturb you again, sir. I have that warrant now.'

'You won't need it,' Braid cheerfully told him. 'I have the key. Mr Messiter was here this morning.' He started to recount the conversation.

'Then I suppose he took out his cutting from *The Times*?' put in the inspector.

'You *know* about that?'

'Do I?' he said caustically. 'The man has been round just about every stamp shop north of Birmingham telling the tale of that young woman and the Penny Blacks on her dressing-room wall.'

Braid frowned. 'There's nothing dishonest in that. The announcement really did appear in *The Times*, didn't it?'

'It did, sir. We checked. And this *is* the address mentioned.' The inspector eyed him expressionlessly. 'The trouble is that the Penny Blacks our friend Messiter has been selling in the north aren't off any dressing-room wall. He buys them from a dealer in London, common specimens, about ten pounds each one. Then he works on them,'

'Works on them? What do you mean?'

'Penny Blacks are valued according to the plates they were printed from, sir. There are distinctive markings on each of the plates, most particularly in the shape of the guide letters that appear in the corners. The stamps Messiter has been selling are doctored to make them appear rare. He buys a common Plate 6 stamp in London, touches up the guide letters and sells it to a Manchester dealer as a Plate 11 stamp for a hundred pounds. As it's catalogued at twice that, the dealer thinks he has a bargain. Messiter picks his victims carefully: generally they aren't specialists in early English stamps, but almost any dealer is ready to look at a Penny Black in case it's a rare one.'

Braid shook his head. 'I don't understand this at all. Why should Messiter have needed to resort to forgery? There are twenty thousand stamps upstairs.'

'Have you seen them?'

'No, but the newspaper announcement – '

'That fools everyone, sir.'

'You said it was genuine.'

'It is. And the idea of a roomful of Penny Blacks excites people's imagination. They *want* to believe it. That's the secret of all the best confidence tricks. Now why do you suppose Messiter had a mortice lock fitted on that room? You thought it was because the contents were worth a fortune? Has it occurred to you as a possibility that he didn't want anyone to know there was nothing there?'

Braid's dream disintegrated.

'It stands to reason, doesn't it,' the inspector went on, 'that the stamps were stripped off the wall generations ago? When Messiter found empty walls, he couldn't abandon the idea. It had taken a grip on him. That young woman who thought of papering her wall with stamps could never have supposed she would be responsible over a century later for turning a man to crime.' He held out his hand. 'If I could have that key, sir, I'd like to see the room for myself.'

Braid followed the inspector upstairs and watched him unlock the door. They entered the room.

'I don't mind admitting I have a sneaking respect for Messiter,' the inspector said. 'Imagine the poor beggar coming in here at last after going to all the trouble he did to find the place. Look, you can see where he peeled back the wallpaper layer by layer' – gripping a furl of paper, he drew it casually aside – 'to find absolutely – ' He stopped. 'My God!'

The stamps were there, neatly pasted in rows.

Braid said nothing, but the blood slowly drained from his face.

Miss E.D.'s scheme of interior decoration had been more ambitious than anyone expected. She had diligently blocked out each stamp in ink – red, blue or green – to form an intricate mosaic. Penny Blacks or Twopence Blues, Plate 6 or Plate 11, they were as she had described them in *The Times*, worthless little articles.

George Milner

THE CARELESS SEA

She was still writing letters, though it was almost time to
start cooking lunch – lunch for James and herself. From
her writing desk in the bow-window of their sheltered
farmhouse she could see him walking, as he often did in
the mornings, along the very edge of the calm sea lapping the sand in their private cove below the house.

This morning his stoop, his gentle pace, the ineffectual-
ness of his walking and his life, exasperated her in a
manner more violent than they ordinarily did. For this
morning she saw him not merely as a habit, an unlucky
but bearable destiny, but as a barrier to the something
better which now offered.

Why, ten years ago, had she married this man? The
usual humiliating answer to this humiliating question was
'Because he was younger', meaning, 'Because we were
both younger and all our judgements suspended by the
force of a physical magnetism', which, she thought, came
to almost the same thing as saying: 'There is no free will,
all is predestined'. And she didn't believe that.

He had had some money – that fact alone absolved her
from part of the charge of sheer physical infatuation, but
what had he done with the money, or what, for that
matter, had he done at all? Nothing. Nothing, nothing.
She had herself seen life as an event in which one takes
part, a sparkling invitation to contribute, to spend, to risk
triumph or disaster. She remembered how, in the fantasies of dreams which were no doubt unhealthy, she had
seen herself as something of a tigress; certainly her big

bones and high, blonde looks helped lessen the absurdity of such fancies. At other times she had seen herself as a stimulus or appendage to greatness, for was not this greatness the thing to be found in life? The shaping of others' lives, the effecting of even a tiny kink in destiny's long coil?

When, after her marriage, she first began to see the pattern of this dilemma, she thought that children would obscure or alleviate it, might even galvanise James into a new attitude or activity. But even there he had failed her. She was sick of gentleness and tolerance and kindness.

It was James's own affair that his life should be a futile waste, but that it should thus affect her own had become, this morning, unbearable. He was always reading, yet he never seemed to gain therefrom, never came to any conclusions. Each new point of view or addition of knowledge to his mind seemed only to become another useless file on the same subject, a layer added to a store of information that had no conceivable value to anybody. She saw no prospect of its ever being put to use – indeed he seemed to drift further into the role of spectator as the years passed. An article or two on birds had been his sole contribution to human activity that she could recognise as such. Birds, she thought, the last thing. There was cause for exasperation.

She saw now that she had only an hour in which to cook lunch, exactly the time it would take her. But she must think, it would have to wait a quarter of an hour, James would notice if it was late but not if she merely omitted the sauce she had intended to make. Not that he would complain either way. He would be gentle, easy, relaxed, maddening.

This was a most extraordinary note Peter had written her, and extremely indiscreet. It said : 'My darling Jane, The divorce is through, as you may have seen, and your admirer is now ready for anything! He has difficulty, though, in getting the image of a very beautiful and magnificent young woman out of his head. My darling girl,

I wish you would agree to tackle the situation – they often yield to onslaughts, you know. Think it over very carefully – and think of your positively bemused admirer – P.'

She didn't mind the tone of his insincerity – she thought they understood each other. But the obscurity was unhelpful. She had met Peter, the young member for a Hampshire constituency, at a cocktail party a year ago, and although there had been nothing between them to which anyone could object there had been a marked significance, sometimes pointedly underlined, in the persistence of his attention to her; he had gone out of his way to keep in touch by an irregular correspondence, had sent her flowers once when she was staying at the flat of a girl-friend in London, evidently to indicate that he had and could find out her movements and was interested in them. Then he had divorced his wife – but how could that be anything to do with her? It was from every point of view ridiculous. But then again, he had bought a summer cottage, only a mile or two along the Devon coast from where James and she lived. She didn't know how much he was there – they scarcely ever met – and yet the thing was curious. Coincidences, you might say, trifles, but they formed a pattern. And now this letter, far more specific than anything that had come from him before, a genuine bombshell.

It was some sort of an invitation to action, she felt convinced. Peter was a man for action. She was being invited to act, and by doing so to share a life of action. Everything could be hers, were it not for James.

She had no grounds whatever for divorcing James, nor could they easily be trumped up. She had no intention of being divorced herself. Would he be prepared to co-operate to the extent of arranging circumstances and allowing her to divorce him? She thought what it would be like having to live with him throughout the years once such a suggestion had been advanced and he had rejected it; of the sympathy and kindness he would show, the puzzled reproachfulness that would sometimes break through. It was not a risk to be taken lightly.

On the beach below she saw his shadow shorten as he bent to lift or examine something in the sand, a shell or other minuscule secretion of the sea. The petty, futile enquiry was going on as it always did, useless grist for a useless mill. She wondered why he could not just dissolve and evaporate, why the physical laws were so drearily constant, why every external ingredient of her trap remained always static. Had the powers that be no resource or invention, could not spring sometimes follow autumn or even winter winter, did the damned things never change? Did they never take sides? Everything was predictable, even the wretched tides and stars could be calculated for years and even centuries ahead, as long as a fool mathematician cared to sit at his logarithms. Was everything predestined, nothing wonderful?

Could he not whisk away to sea and vanish?

It occurred to her that perhaps he could, that here was the thing that was meant by action, that every one of us could take his cue when the poet said that our fates are not in our stars but in ourselves.

There was this about the constant laws – that at least water could be relied on to drown a man.

She supposed that they would be going sailing that afternoon in James's dinghy, as they most often did on summer afternoons when the wind was moderate; today it blew strongly enough. Far out, alone in the ocean, they would bathe by turns, while the other sailed on single-handed with the dinghy, tacking nearby until a hail from the head bobbing, a solitary object in the sea, would convey the wish to be picked up. She loved the clean feel of the open sea about her, its power and buoyancy; she loved the sense of solitude, more potent here than she had ever known it; once she had loved, too, the sense of dependence on the man whose hand held the dinghy's tiller, who at such times, with the ocean and freedom all his, was held to the pledge to pick her up again only by his love, who could be relied on not only to wait and come back but to fight, should any mishap have occurred, for her body. Her habit had been simply to discard her clothes and jump overboard, filled with the excitement of the thing and of their relationship, but she now saw it as charactertisic of James that he should always solemnly have donned his bathing trunks out there in the windy spaces.

Lately, the absolute dependence of the swimmer in the water upon the partner who sailed the boat had come more often to the forefront of her mind. It had occurred to her often that, should she steer away, the wind blowing her softly homeward on a straight course through the lapping wavelets, the distance between James and herself would grow in inverse ratio to the dwindling years, days and minutes of his life, so that by the time she moored near the farmhouse the life should be failing fast. A sailing accident was even better than a shooting accident, so little could really be made of it afterwards: these things happened, everyone knew; what could a woman be expected to do when some disaster befell her husband sailing? Grapple single-handed with the ocean?

She thought that it would do, and she also thought that too protracted contemplation of a challenge once formulated could prove enfeebling or even unbalancing. She went to cook the lunch.

The sun was still high in the west when she sailed round the point alone, and into the bay of her own little cove. She must be quick about mooring, getting ashore in the rowing-boat, reaching the telephone, in case anyone should be overlooking the narrow cove – not that this was likely. Leave the sails up, not bother with them this once – that would show her hurry. Then to appear rattled, though here her confidence in her own pent-up powers merged with the feeling of genuine disturbance she had felt since hearing the last faint, bewildered cry at the greatest distance a voice would carry through the wind and above the sea. In the opening of her new life she would exorcise that memory.

'There's been an accident – a terrible accident.' What a fool she felt on the telephone – one might have thought the thing was done, an act complete in itself without these trimmings. 'Cramps – couldn't catch hold of him – turned over so fast – too soon – oh, I can't bear to think of it – too soon after lunch, perhaps?'

For the very first time it occurred to her to wonder what Peter would make of it.

The police came and were kind. They said the rescue launches and lifeboats were searching, had gone out at once. They shook their heads, and she saw that they believed her; she determined that no vanity in this second success should reveal itself in her manner; nothing, now, but to play it down and let it tail away as the plight of the widow bereaved.

In the late evening she sat alone in the dark, silent farmhouse, not reading, but sometimes smoking, and gazing into the fire. She had forced herself to eat, for did she not see more eating in future, more *living*, and was this not also a problem to be grappled and started on at once?

She was woken from her reverie by the sound of a car, and again disposed herself to behave sadly, quietly, mousily, and answer questions.

Then came footsteps, but there was no ring on the bell: she heard the front door open, and did not like this, though it was a stray impression of hers, gained from books, that policemen on their way to an arrest were always meticulously polite. It was a nasty moment, because who could this be if not policemen? No relatives could be swarming round her yet. And there was no one else resident in the house, no one near with the right to open the door and walk in as though the place belonged to them. It belonged, after all, to her.

It sounded like two people, and she heard a man's voice. Policemen, surely? Surely not thieves, that would be too terrible a coincidence, though if so she would contrive to meet that too.

Peter opened the door. She could not understand his look – it was so unlike him.

Then James came in, wearing no clothes of his own. He was paler than usual, stooped more than ever, and he, too, wore a look she did not recognise.

She rushed forward and threw her arms round him and said :

'Oh, James, darling, you had cramps, I couldn't catch hold of you – oh, I thought you'd drowned.'

'Yes,' he said, and there was something new in the gentle tones. 'I had cramps.'

He held her away from him and his brown eyes looked into hers. She felt his grip to be stronger than she had ever known it, as though the sea had somehow changed the man.

She wondered if she were not dreaming all this, for she knew it was impossible for James to be here, or in this world. The sea had been so empty where she left him. He was flesh and blood, though.

'Come by the fire,' she said. 'I'll get you a hot drink. And one for Peter, too. I could do with one myself.'

The men said nothing, but they settled by the fire. She brought drinks in, and sat on the floor at James's feet so that she could stroke his knee.

It was touch and go now, she thought, a question of what, if anything, could be saved – unless she were dreaming.

She thought there was something terrible about their silence, and said :

'Darling . . . you must tell me about how you were rescued, if you can bear to. I'd given up hope, I can hardly believe it.'

'You mustn't be impatient,' said Peter.

'But I think she has every right to be,' said James slowly. And then he sat for minutes in silence again.

She thought perhaps she was really going mad. Yet her

faculties answered her that both these men were flesh and blood, common men returning after an adventure.

'Tell me,' she said, fondling his knee.

'It was quite simple,' he said. 'The fishing boat picked me up.'

But there had been no fishing boat, not a sign of one in all the empty sea.

'The fishing boat,' she said blankly.

'It was very close,' he said. 'I thought you must have seen it.'

She brushed a hand across her forehead and her eyes.

'What . . . did it look like?'

'It had black sails – I don't think you can have missed it, Jane. Otherwise you wouldn't have left me – I mean, you'd have waited, I might have shown up again.'

'Yes,' she said. 'How idiotic of me. It's been such a terrible day – of course I saw it. What were the men like in it, though? Were they kind?'

'They picked me up,' he said. 'They were just men.'

Peter said:

'I must go now – I only brought him home because he wanted to come.'

She went out into the hall with him.

'This is goodbye,' he said. 'I shan't need the cottage any more.'

'Please . . .' she said. 'Please, Peter.'

'I often watched you two out there, you know. I had binoculars. I wanted to be one of the partners in the idyll I used to see.'

'You could still be.'

'I think you're going mad,' he said. 'It served you right about the black sails.'

He went out.

Through her bitter bewilderment she knew only one thing: that it must be the sea that had failed her, that for once had taken sides.

She steeled herself to go back into the sitting room. Once there she said wildly:

'Why were the sails black?'

'I'm sorry, my dear,' he said. 'They had to be some colour. I thought it would make them sound real.'

Real.

He went on, 'Did I choose a bad colour? I'm sorry, my dear, I only wanted to help us along with . . . with some kind of story.'

It had been sheer, stupid kindness.

Michael Sinclair

THE YOUNG DUTCHMAN

They pulled him out from among the frozen garbage by
the door of the Garden of Eden massage parlour and
brought him to the Seventeenth Precinct House on Fifty-
First Street. The cop, O'Connor, had found him just after
midnight and the Precinct House was the nearest place
to take him. That was when they still thought they might
save him. Later, they wrapped the body in a black water-
proof sheet, strapped it up and left it for the ambulance.
It would be taken to the morgue in due course, but on
a busy night, the quick came before the dead.

O'Connor and one of the desk cops worked through
the phone numbers in the dead man's diary. At two in
the morning no one wanted to know and they were only
half through when Lieutenant Flamini from Homicide
came in.

'Who is it?'

'A Peter van Damm,' said O'Connor. He was a big
traditional Irishman who had little time for Homicide
and less for the sallow Italianate wisp of a man that
Flamini was.

'What was he?'

'Don't know nothin' yet.'

'Motive?'

'Mugging, drugs, male hooker – found round from
Fifty-Third Street remember . . .'

'Which?'

'Don't know. Still had his wallet and watch so I'd . . .'

'Let me see him.' Flamini took off his gloves, folded

them neatly in his hands, and watched without expression as O'Connor uncovered the body.

'Pierced right ear. Big tear. Ring or whatever he was wearin' ripped out. See . . . flecks of blood.' O'Connor jabbed with a blunt index finger.

'I can see, thank you,' said Flamini precisely.

'Fur coat on and that ear . . . Real queen. Early twenties. Musta been a faggot . . . Okay?'

'That's not just fur. That's mink.'

'Outa my class. How d'ya know?'

'Flamini furs: I'm the family black sheep. That's six thousand dollars of coat.'

'No kiddin'?'

'No kidding,' echoed Flamini.

Three phone numbers later they woke Janie Morris. When they said the name she hung up abruptly but arrived from East Eighty-Ninth Street a bare twenty minutes later. O'Connor unveiled the body. She did not show emotion, turning only a fraction more drawn – a white unmade-up face under the hastily brushed hair. She would be in her late thirties, heavy, not unattractive in a sullen animal way.

O'Connor led her into the green and tile interrogation room that smelled of roach powder. Flamini stood waiting with a duty stenographer. She spoke in a hesitant monologue, anticipating questions before they were put to her. Flamini let her talk without interruption.

'Janie Morris, actress . . . No, not working at the moment. . . . Yes, resting that's what they do call it. And he's . . . he was Peter van Damm. A friend . . . No, no. Flamboyant, effeminate but not gay. No . . . no . . . I am sure. He lived with me . . . lived with me a long time; nearly eighteen months . . . until last week. Drugs . . ? Did you say drugs? Well, well a little of the soft . . . yes grass . . . very occasionally. Never the hard. No, that wasn't Peter's line. I wouldn't have allowed it. Allowed it . . ? Yes, I suppose I always did tell him what to do.

I was older of course. He relied on me in a lot of ways. Money? Did you say money? Don't make me laugh. Peter had more money than everyone else I know put together. . . . Came from his family. No, I . . . His father's something important in Holland. No, I don't know what he does. He came over here last summer to see Peter, but I decided, Peter and I decided, that it would be better if I stayed in the background. We never met. No, nothing more, I'm afraid. He has a sister too somewhere . . . but . . . Peter didn't talk about his family much.'

She dried up and stared emptily at the cracked green wall in front of her through half-closed, puffy eyes.

'What did he do?' Flamini probed gently after a few moments of silence. Like a psychiatrist, he did not want to break the flow.

'Student. It started off as architecture, then it was interior design, then . . . then there was very little studying. He hadn't been brought up to work. I'd try to make him, tease him, force him, bribe him. He'd sit in front of an open textbook . . . sitting, not dreaming. He had no real ambitions beyond going to the next party.'

'And you broke up?'

'Last week. Last Sunday.'

'Why?'

She hesitated. 'He said he was moving out. No reasons. Out of the blue. He was going to live with a friend in the Village. He didn't explain. I didn't ask. It was going to come sometime. I had got used to having him around but he could pall at times. Self-centred. No great intellectual; no great conversationalist was Peter.' She paused for a moment, then, 'How was it done? How did he . . .?'

'One shot. Very close range. The heart. . . And you say, Miss Morris, that he wasn't gay? Who was his friend?'

'Don't know his friend. A man, another Dutchman, I think. He rang once. No, Peter wasn't homosexual.'

'Mink coat and a pierced ear,' said Flamini.

'That fur coat was mink was it? He'd had it all the

135

time he was with me. But a pierced ear? You said a pierced ear? I know every inch of him. He doesn't have a pierced ear, Lieutenant.'

'He does now,' said Flamini.

'He wouldn't have done that. He wouldn't do that to his body. Cultivating a perfect body was his only hobby.' Janie Morris looked straight at Lieutenant Flamini as if seeing him for the first time.

'He did. Or somebody did. D'you want to see again?'

'No,' said Janie Morris. The word came out fast and hard.

Flamini sent her home in a squad car. The after-shock had begun to show through the numbing anaesthetic which had been her first reaction to the death. When that sort of thing happened, the lieutenant knew to break off. He was master of the cold, unfashionable art of interrogation.

Flamini's alternative career would have been as a mathematician. He took all the prizes at his Brooklyn school but after a brief spell with the Army in South-East Asia, he had a need for more action, more discipline than teaching would give. So just as he had broken the family tradition and braved his father's anger by abandoning the fur trade, so he later horrified his mother and nearly everyone else he knew by joining New York's Finest. He had done well and fast. A smooth meticulous logic, a passion for detail, a fascination with the human mind had brought him considerable success. He stood apart from the big men – big physically, big in behaviour, who comprised the bulk of his colleagues in the force. The minimum permissible height, fragile looking, though with a lithe toughness when need be, he was always elegantly even dapperly dressed. Unmarried; thirty-eight, with numerous nice Brooklyn girls always around him.

At ten the next morning he arrived at Janie Morris's apartment on Eighty-Ninth and Lexington. A well judged gestation period between interviews was crucial to

136

his whole approach : she would have slept a little but not too much.

Small, but well kept rooms; lots of signed glossy photographs of the stars; two bedrooms. 'We shared mostly, but sometimes he would move into the spare room,' she explained. 'We never quarrelled. He just went.'

'Any belongings still here?'

'Architecture and design books. A few student notes. A suitcase – nothing in it except clothes. I just checked.'

'You should have left that for us.'

'Sorry. I didn't . . .'

'He carried this address book. Any of these names familiar?'

She thumbed through the battered little book and gave him a running commentary on the ones she knew. Few seemed of obvious note though he would have them all checked out to see if any had seen Peter van Damm in the past week.

'He was moving to Greenwich Village?'

'That's what he told me.'

'Two addresses are in the Village. Know either?'

'No.'

'You've been helpful, Miss Morris.' Pulling his gloves on, Flamini moved to the door. She started to say something, then hesitated.

'What is it?'

'You're going down to the Village now?'

'Yes.'

'If I came too, I . . . I might be of some . . . Check things out on the spot. You know . . . I'd like to help.'

'Why not. Get your coat. I'll be waiting in the car down below.'

The first address was a run-down apartment block in MacDougall Street. Lieutenant Flamini and Janie Morris, accompanied by a uniformed cop, arrived at the door of the apartment at the same time as a large fat man who, carrying two heavy suitcases, was sweating profusely despite the stale coldness of the air in the passageway. Seeing the three congregating behind him as he searched for his keys, the man turned and exclaimed: 'Oh Jesus. Just what I needed. Cops. Burgled while I've been away, that it?'

'Not so,' said Flamini. 'You the owner of this apartment? Mr Reuben?'

'I'm Joe Reuben.'

'Flamini. N.Y.P.D. How long you been away Mr Reuben?'

'Four weeks.'

'Where?'

'Look, we can go inside. The neighbours . . . What's all this about?'

'Where?' repeated the lieutenant.

'Orlando, Florida.'

'You know a Peter van Damm?'

'No. I . . .'

'Your name's in his address book.'

'Wait a minute. Good-looking Dutch boy. Twenty, twenty-five?'

'Right.'

'Yeah. Met him at a party. Months ago.'

'Since then?'

'Never seen him.'

'Sure?'

'Sure, I'm sure. Look I got his address somewhere. Maybe it could help. He's shacked up with some old hag of a would-be actress up in the Eighties somewhere.'

'No need, Mr Reuben. Sorry to disturb you,' said Lieutenant Flamini quietly.

He avoided looking at Janie Morris as they left the building. 'You sure you want to stick with us, Miss Morris?'

'Yes. Don't worry, Lieutenant. I've been called worse.'

'I wouldn't pay . . .'

'The trouble is that remark must have come from Peter. That hurts more.'

The other address was a loft in the East Village: a prosperous looking approach and a magnificent oak front door. Flamini pressed the bell. Nothing happened. He pressed again. A voice switched on through a small intercom above the bell.

'Who is it?'

'Police. To see Mr Stoepman.'

'Oh . . . Police did you say? Just a minute. I'm in my bath.'

Two minutes later, a middle-aged man, totally bald and wrapped in an orange towelling robe, opened the door. To judge by his bright pink face, the bath had been very hot.

'My . . . Quite a delegation. What can I do?' He had a slight accent which Flamini couldn't place.

'May we come in?'

'Yes, well . . . May I see some form of identification?'

Flamini produced his card and Stoepman, somewhat reluctantly, led them into a magnificent loft room, beautifully panelled and furnished in the best conception of modern taste.

'I compliment you, Mr Stoepman.'

'Yes, well . . . What can I do for you?'

'Peter van Damm.'

'Yes. Peter's not here right now.'

'When did you last see him?'

'Wednesday. Wednesday morning.'

'He was staying here?'

'Look what's all this?'

'Mr van Damm was found dead around midnight last night. Shot.'

'Peter . . .'

'Shot in the chest. Apparently not a robbery . . .'

'Oh, my God. His sister . . . Alma will . . . and how am I going to tell his father? I was meant to be keeping an eye on him. . . . Yes, he stayed here two, three nights.'

'I'd like a statement from you.'

'No statement. No statement.' Stoepman was pacing up and down distraught.

'I must have a statement Mr Stoepman. Here or at Headquarters?'

Stoepman pulled himself together. 'I'll have to take advice. You'll have to come to the Mission, Lieutenant . . . ? Lieutenant . . . ?'

'Flamini's the name, Mr Stoepman. Now please get dressed and come.'

'You don't understand, Lieutenant. I'm Counsellor at the Netherlands Mission to the United Nations. I am a diplomat.'

'Are you claiming some sort of immunity?'

'No, no. Nothing like that. I'm not being charged, I take it? Our rules say we have to make statements with someone else from the Mission . . . I'll want one of my colleagues to be present. My Ambassador will . . . Oh, God . . . My Ambassador will . . .'

'What's the matter, Walter? Who are these people?' A film-star blonde in her mid-twenties, also wrapped in a towel bathrobe, appeared at a doorway.

'Oh, my God, Alma. Police. It's Peter.'

'What's with Peter?' She too had that slight accent.

Stoepman began looking for words so Flamini stepped in. 'Found dead early this morning. Shot once in the chest. Who are you?'

'She's visiting us here. She's . . .' Stoepman began. He was wheezing slightly. It sounded like asthma.

'I'm Peter's sister,' the girl said coldly. Then after a pause: 'Well it's hard but true. He had it coming to him, the life he led.'

From behind him Flamini heard Janie's bitter voice: 'What exactly d'you mean by that?'

Peter van Damm's sister, assuming her to be a police-woman, responded direct. 'Living to no purpose; wild friends; no drive; no discipline; always over-dressed like a millionaire pimp; living with some ancient whore . . .'

140

'Just you . . .' Janie Morris advanced to pass Flamini but he reached out and grabbed her arm.

'Quiet,' he said, 'or you're off this case.'

'Okay, okay. This is my day for home truths,' muttered Janie.

'Who is this woman? What's all this about?' asked Stoepman huskily.

'Are we talking? Are you going to give us a statement?' Flamini was folding and unfolding his gloves in restless hands.

'At the Mission. Later.'

'But I'll talk now,' said the blonde girl, coming forward.

'No, Alma. You mustn't.'

Alma began to speak rapidly to Stoepman in a language Flamini took to be Dutch. Stoepman tried to interrupt but she began shouting at him. After a while he shrugged his shoulders with resignation and plumped himself down breathlessly in a deep leather armchair. 'She can do and say what the hell she likes. Like she always does,' he said.

'Okay, Mr Policeman,' Alma began. 'What do you want to know?'

'You last saw him Wednesday morning?'

'Yes. I had not seen him much since I arrived in New York last week. We had little to say . . . We had breakfast together.'

'He went out after that?'

'He was going to collect some of his things from the woman . . . from where he had been staying.' As she spoke, Alma glanced for a moment at Janie Morris. Perhaps she had guessed who the other woman was.

'And when he didn't reappear?'

'That was Peter's style.'

'Enemies?'

'He wasn't important . . . was never positive enough to have enemies.'

'You're very harsh towards your brother.'

'He was wasted. He wasted himself. He could have done so much. It's been going on for so long that it's difficult to care now.'

'When he was found, he was wearing a mink coat.'

'He always did.'

'And his right ear was newly pierced.'

'Peter would never have the courage to have his ear pierced. It would have spoiled his beauty.'

'Now we're getting somewhere,' said Lieutenant Flamini.

'Well, Miss Morris?' They were going north along East River Drive. Flamini was sitting beside her in the rear seat.

'Yes?' She was staring vacantly out of the window at the fast flowing river.

'Reactions, Miss Morris? I didn't bring you along for the ride.'

'Peter only mentioned her once. He couldn't understand why she hated him so.'

'Why did she?'

'I dunno. He had everything. He always had. He felt it was his birthright, that the world owed him everything. Particularly his father.'

'And?'

'And he owed nothing in return. Unless you love someone very much, Lieutenant, that's hell to live with. At times I would have said his sister had a point.'

It was around eight that same night. Armed with photographs provided by Janie Morris, Homicide had checked out every professional ear-piercer in the Village and all the other names in Peter van Damm's address book. Every way they drew a blank in filling the time gap between the Wednesday breakfast with his sister and the discovery of his body. Then came the call from the Airport. The Immigration Authorities had called in the J.F.K. Airport police and together they picked up a

Libyan student who was booked on the evening Air France flight to Paris. He had been behaving strangely in the Customs hall and they were on high alert over the tip-off about a possible hijack. A search revealed nothing and they had been about to let him go when they found an American Express card belonging to Peter van Damm in his wallet. An alert Airport policeman had spotted the name as being on the daily check-list circulated by Homicide.

'Name?' asked Flamini when he was brought to him later.

'I gave already.' The Libyan looked as scared as he was unshaven.

'Hard or difficult?'

'What you mean?'

'We hold you till you talk. It won't be pleasant. You won't like your stay. You understand?'

'Understand.'

'Name?'

'Hamdi. Ibraihim Hamdi.'

'Tell me more.'

'I want to see Libyan Consul.'

There was a metal table in the centre of the interrogation room. Hamdi was seated on a folding chair on one side, Flamini stood opposite him.

'I want your story. What are you doing here? How d'you have this credit card in your possession?'

There was a long silence. Suddenly Flamini reached forward, grabbed the edge of the metal table and knocked it over on the concrete floor with a resounding crash. Hamdi leapt back terrified but untouched.

'Accidents happen, Mr Hamdi. Accidents happen.' A wisp of a smile played across Flamini's lips for a moment and then was gone. He preferred subtler techniques but only with subtler people.

Whatever happened in that interrogation room immediately thereafter, by ten p.m. Hamdi was talking. Talking non-stop. He'd been a back-up, only a back-up. The others had split and left the U.S. earlier. He had been told to stay on to monitor reactions. Three others had kidnapped Peter van Damm as he came back to Janie Morris's apartment on Wednesday morning to pick up the rest of his belongings. They'd held him all that day until late at night in a rooming house on West Forty-Third Street, waiting for a reply to their ultimatum. The son of the Dutch Minister of the Interior was a magnificent catch. It had taken a long time to plan and it had to be worth it. They'd made Peter talk on the telephone. They'd made him scream down the telephone, a razor-sharp stiletto pierced through his ear, threatening to cut it off and send it as proof that they meant business. Peter van Damm's life in exchange for five P.L.O. freedom fighters, one Japanese Red Army terrorist and two of the Baader-Meinhof Group, held in Dutch jails for hijacking and other crimes. One young man's life for the freedom of seven young men and one young woman. The three kidnappers had intended to play it slow, to give the Dutch authorities time to consider their demands, but they panicked, moved to another hideout on the upper West Side and phoned their demands once again. This time the leader was even more vicious, more threatening. Peter was pleading, weeping, begging with his abductors to leave him his life. Two long days elapsed. The three set a final deadline. They heard nothing. There was no attempt to bargain, no attempt to contact them through their pre-planned go-between. Peter van Damm died at the hands of their cold fury.

'What more d'you want from me?' Janie Morris sat huddled defenceless in a chair in the corner of her living room. It was two in the morning, and had Lieutenant Flamini been a sadist, he might have relished her sexual vulnerability. As it was, he was only using the sensory deprivation experienced by anyone newly wakened from sleep to further his enquiries. It was standard practice.

'He was being held hostage to put pressure on his father.'

'You said that already.'

'They got no response. None.'

'The Dutch didn't even try to bargain?' For a moment she seemed genuinely curious.

'Not as far as I am aware.'

'But I don't know anything.'

'They negotiated . . . they were negotiating with a woman. Hamdi knew that much.'

'Not me, Lieutenant. Not me.'

'So who was the go-between?'

'You're the detective, Lieutenant.'

Flamini picked up his gloves from a side table and stood up. 'I hope I haven't disturbed your sleep too much, Miss Morris,' he said.

Flamini guessed that it would take longer, but it was only just dawn when Janie Morris left her apartment and took a cab to the Village. He waited five minutes, then rang Stoepman's bell. The sister opened the door immediately. There was no sign of Stoepman.

'We'd make a good team, Miss Morris. Detective work plus a woman's hunch,' he said, entering the luxurious room unasked. 'Now I have to speak to Miss van Damm alone.'

'This woman can stay if she wants, so long as you take her with you when you go. I've told her I have absolutely nothing to say to her. Nothing much to you either, Mr Policeman.'

'Let's try, shall we? You were telephoned repeatedly by the kidnappers.'

'What kidnappers?'

'One of them's booked. He's made a full statement.'

'And?'

'And you let them kill your brother.' Flamini heard from behind him, Janie Morris's sharp intake of breath. 'Peter van Damm was kidnapped to exert pressure on your father. They wanted to exchange him for eight terrorists held in prison in Holland. Right so far?'

There was a long silence, then: 'Which shows what fools they were,' the sister spat out the words.

'They telephoned you here.'

'Yes, but Mr Stoepman was away. He knows nothing.'

'You passed their messages on to your father?'

'Why should I? At first I thought it was some sort of joke. Who would bother with Peter? Then . . . my father's position . . . my father's career . . . Peter was a nothing. My father has enough troubles. In any case it would not have been his decision alone. The Dutch Government are tough on terrorism. You know that, Mr Policeman. They would not have given in. My father would only have had the double agony . . .'

'So you took the decision for him, and for your country.'

'If you like to put it so grandly.'

'But then you might just have persuaded your father. He might just have brought his colleagues round.'

'Go ahead, Mr Policeman. Charge me. It will be less painful than listening to your moralising.'

The Commissioner of Police of New York City had Stoepman and another man with him.

'This is His Excellency the Netherlands Ambassador to the United Nations – Lieutenant Flamini from Homicide. You know Mr Stoepman.'

The Ambassador inclined his head slightly but did not proffer his hand. Stoepman was staring down at his feet.

'How is it going?' continued the Commissioner.

'I believe we've got a case, Sir.'

'Tell us about it, Lieutenant . . . Yes, Lieutenant . . . you can speak freely in front of the Ambassador.'

Flamini went through the whole affair. He had his notes with him but did not refer to them. He was a methodical man and at times like this he had total recall. He took about ten minutes and the others heard him out in silence. The Commissioner looked tired; the Ambassador showed little emotion; Stoepman however was no actor and his pink face betrayed a range of horrified feeling with his asthmatic breathing as backdrop to Flamini's words.

'It's a delicate business, Lieutenant. The State Department . . .' When Flamini finished, the Commissioner responded with unaccustomed hesitancy.

'What are you telling me, Commissioner?'

'Nothing, Lieutenant. Nothing. Thank you for your report. If you would wait outside, I'd like to have a further word with you after His Excellency and Mr Stoepman have left.'

Half an hour later Flamini was back with the Commissioner. The latter was another big cop, big in every way: solid, dependable, with a heavy, creased, likeable face.

'Okay, son. Say . . . what's your first name, Flamini?'

'Leo, Commissioner.'

'Okay, Leo. You're a good officer. Great record. Just seen your file. Now . . . now we've got something here that's very delicate.'

'Obviously.'

'State Department were on to me.'

'You said.'

'That murder was a mugging.'

'No, it wasn't, Commissioner. It . . . couldn't be. Hamdi's evidence. The sister . . . You should see the body.'

'I have, Leo. I have.'

'You have?' Flamini showed his astonishment. Commissioners did not usually spend much time in the mortuary.

'And the case is closed. Shut hard. Shred the file. I don't want to hear no more . . .'

'But . . .'

'And no "buts". I don't want no lectures on morality from you. Before you leave this room, Leo, you're going to believe . . . to know it was a mugging too. Just like I do. A good old-fashioned no-bones-about-it New York mugging.'

'Why, Commissioner?'

'Because I say so, Lieutenant Leo Flamini. Because I say so.'

The case died then. Lieutenant Flamini was a good officer, he valued the truth but he was no rebel to authority. There's plenty of work for Homicide in New York City and he moved quickly on to deal with a drug pusher found strangled on the Lower East Side. He was only a little perturbed at having the van Damm case closed before its due time.

Ten days later he was again at the Seventeenth Precinct House on Fifty-First Street working on some case files.

The Irish cop, O'Connor came in. 'Call for you, Lieutenant. Someone by the name of Stepman or somethin'!'

Flamini thought for a moment, then took the phone. 'Mr Stoepman . . . ?'

'Flamini? Is that you? . . . Yes? . . . Thank God. It's Alma . . . Peter van Damm's sister. She's gone . . . We've had a phone call It's the same group . . . Yes . . . Yes . . . damn you, we're sure of it. We're on to the State Department of course. Can you get the Commissioner to ring my Ambassador? Urgently, please, urgently.'

'Thank you for letting me know, Mr Stoepman. We'll be in touch.' Flamini replaced the receiver, picked up his gloves and slowly left the room.

June Thomson

CROSSING BRIDGES

When Charlie's widow came back penniless from South
America, nobody knew what to do with her. It was out
of the question that she should go to Charlie's mother.
Mrs Stapleton had problems of her own; or, rather, one
special problem of many years' standing for which she was
having drying-out treatment yet again in a clinic on the
east coast, while Charlie's father had long since disappeared – to the Bahamas, so some of the family said,
where he was supposed to be living in considerable ease
and comfort with a mistress half his age.

There were cousins and aunts, of course, who were
prepared to put her up for a weekend or even a week or
two but no one could offer her a more permanent home
and so, in the end, she fetched up at Dorothy Linton's
who, after all, had that big house just to herself most of
the time now that her daughter had a job and a flat of
her own in London.

Dorothy was in two minds, as she was about most
things, about offering hospitality to Charlie's widow when
Arthur Bailey, Charlie's uncle who was an accountant
and who had taken it on himself to sort out the girl's
affairs, suggested it. Dorothy had been very fond of
Charlie and, as his godmother and a lifelong friend of
Barbara Stapleton, had often had him to stay with her
when things had been especially difficult at home. In
fact, she had come to look on him as family; almost as
the son she had never had. There had even been a time

when she had hoped that he and her daughter Margot might have married. Dorothy was convinced Margot had loved him, although she had never spoken of her feelings. She was one of those uncommunicative, practical girls, forever doing something useful, like exercising the dogs; a cover-up, Dorothy liked to feel, for deep emotions. As for Charlie, he had always been his charming, amusing self, played a lot of tennis with Margot, teased her, even helped her with the dogs, and then, to everyone's surprise and consternation, had suddenly married a young girl he met in Bath, practically out of the school-room, whisking her away from under her guardian's nose to a registry office wedding in London and then to Brazil where four years later he had so tragically died. No one in the family had met the girl. Not even his mother had gone to the wedding although, to be fair to Charlie, Barbara Stapleton hadn't been in a fit state at the time to attend anything.

He had written, of course, to the family and to Dorothy. She still had his letter in her dressing-table drawer where she kept her mementoes; such a charmingly frank letter, typical of dear Charlie, explaining that it had been love at first sight – 'like being showered with stars' – a delightfully romantic statement that made her forgive any lingering disappointment for Margot's lost chances; after all, she couldn't imagine Margot inspiring such celestial passion – and going on to say that he and what was the girl's name? – Juliet? Perdita? – some Shakespearian heroine, anyway – were blissfully happy.

Then nothing much except for cards at Christmas until the dreadful news of his death from a heart attack.

And now here was his widow standing in Dorothy's hall, looking lost and shy and incredibly young, really little more than a child, with fair hair tied back with a black ribbon and a face like a pale flower, and the awful thing was Dorothy couldn't remember her name. She really should have thought to read Charlie's letter again before she arrived, especially as the girl seemed to know so much about her.

'You're Charlie's godmother, Aunt Doe. Charlie spoke so often about you and the house,' she said, looking about her and smiling softly. 'The orchard and the lawn where he used to play croquet and the tree house. He always said he spent the happiest days of his childhood here. It seems so awful that he had to die for us to meet.'

It was said with such brave, sweet, gentle sadness that Dorothy Linton opened her arms and folded the girl to her heart.

Jessica, as she discovered later, re-reading Charlie's letter in bed; orphaned at twelve and brought up by an unsympathetic bachelor uncle who had promptly packed her off to boarding school and finally washed his hands of her on her marriage.

'You'd love her if only you could meet her, Aunt Doe,' Charlie had written. 'She's like something out of a fairy tale, all gold and gossamer, and so trusting and loving. I think that's what made me fall in love with her – her childlike need to be cherished.'

He was perfectly right. Jessica needed love; mothering really, perhaps from losing her own mother at such an impressionable age, and Dorothy responded happily to this need with all the maternal touches she was so good at – fresh flowers in her room, breakfast in bed, tea taken together in the garden, that had made Margot so impatient in the past, evoking cries of, 'Oh, Mother, don't fuss so much!'

Jessica made no such protest to Dorothy's delight, although her happiness was clouded sometimes by vague feelings of guilt on Margot's account. Take the matter of the bedroom, for instance. It seemed kinder to offer her Margot's. It was larger and sunnier than the spare room with a pleasant view over the garden but, as she cleared out the remainder of Margot's possessions from the drawers and cupboards, the last remnants of her old life at home that she had either forgotten to throw away or take with her to London, Dorothy felt a twinge of conscience.

Not that she did it without ringing up Margot to get her consent, even if it was after Jessica had moved in. Not that it was ever very satisfactory to talk to Margot on the telephone. She always sounded impatient, as if the call had disturbed her in the middle of something important, as probably it had, for Margot often said that her work as a probation officer gave her hardly a moment to herself. To compensate and out of a nervous reaction, Dorothy always found herself becoming too talkative and effusive.

She did it now, explaining about Jessica.

'You see, darling, there's no money. Not a penny. It seems Charlie had been unwise about his investments and when he died everything had to be sold to pay off his debts. Even her engagement ring.'

Jessica had told her this the first evening she arrived, weeping a little when she spoke about the ring. She seemed to mind its loss more than the house and the furniture. But there had been no word of blame against Charlie, Jessica insisting that he had been badly advised.

'So I said she could come here for the time being until everything can be sorted out,' Dorothy added. 'And I'm afraid I've done something dreadfully naughty.'

For a ridiculous moment, she felt their roles were reversed and it was she who was the child owning up to the parent.

'For goodness' sake, what is it?' Margot asked impatiently.

'I've let her have your room,' Dorothy confessed.

There was a small silence that Dorothy found impossible to read. Was Margot angry? Or hurt? Or simply indifferent?

'You see, darling, the spare bedroom needs redecorating and I thought . . .'

She was going to add that, as Margot came home so

152

infrequently, there was no point in leaving it empty, only that might sound like complaining, the last thing Dorothy wanted to do. After all, Margot had her own life to live now, as she so often told herself.

'Of course, she can always move out if you need it,' she hastened to add.

'Oh, I can kip down anywhere. It really doesn't matter. Don't worry about me,' Margot replied with an off-handedness that wasn't entirely convincing. 'I must go now, mother. I've got dozens of reports to write up.'

And she rang off before Dorothy could even say good-bye, although she took care to replace the receiver with gentle conciliation.

So, despite the telephone conversation, the bedroom continued to be a source of unease, as did her increasing enjoyment of Jessica's company. They got on so well together that soon the question of Jessica's departure was no longer a topic of discussion as it had been in the first few days after her arrival. It had been suggested then that Jessica might get a job and a flat of her own as soon as her affairs were sorted out and learn to be independent. But, as Jessica herself admitted in one of those little candid outbursts that Dorothy found so brave and endearing, there wasn't much she was skilled at except making a home for a husband.

At that she must have been excellent, Dorothy thought. She had all the qualities that a man like Charlie would have admired in a woman. She was gentle, sweet-natured, malleable and very pretty, especially now that she was losing the wan look she had had when she first arrived and was beginning to recover her bloom, and so appreciative of everything that was done for her.

It delighted Dorothy to buy her presents; underwear, a pair of white sandals, a long, flowered skirt that they had seen and admired in a shop window in Long Barton; small gifts that really cost very little and made the girl so happy although, like the bedroom, Dorothy had uneasy moments about them. In some way that she couldn't explain, she felt she was depriving Margot, although Margot had never cared much for clothes and certainly wouldn't have wanted anything so pretty and feminine.

But behind these instances of unease lay a much deeper sense of guilt that Dorothy didn't care to examine too closely although, as the days passed, she found less easy to ignore. The truth was Jessica was taking over in her heart the place Margot should have occupied; should have, because Margot had never been close to her even as a child, squirming away from any demonstrations of affection, offering a cool cheek only to be kissed and later, through her difficult, brooding adolescence, spending as little time as possible in her mother's company, lying sprawled out on her bed reading when she wasn't out with the dogs or playing tennis or taking long, solitary bike rides round the countryside, sketching churches, so she said, for her art class at school, although Dorothy had never once seen any product from these excursions.

Whereas Jessica offered all the companionship and affection that Dorothy craved. They shopped and went to the hairdresser's together or for country drives in the car. Jessica helped, too, with the church flowers when it was Dorothy's turn on the rota or picked raspberries with her from the garden for mousse on Sundays, while the evenings were spent playing cards or reading or indulging in easy, desultory conversation and laughter. And when they finally parted for the night, Jessica always kissed her with warm affection, nuzzling her soft cheek against Dorothy's.

When Margot's telephone call came it was like a douche of cold water.

'I shall be coming down on Saturday,' she announced briskly.

'Oh, darling, how splendid!' Dorothy cried enthusiastically, although she felt a small sinking of the heart at the news. 'How long for? Just the weekend?'

'No, for four or five days. I've got some leave due to me and it doesn't seem worth going away anywhere. It's too late now to book anyway so I thought I might as well come home.'

It did cross Dorothy's mind that it might have been expressed more graciously. She also had the uneasy feeling that Margot was coming home in order to check up on her.

'Your room . . .' she began faintly.

Again there was one of those silences that Dorothy was only too familiar with and then Margot asked abruptly, 'Do you mean she's still there with you?'

'Well, yes,' Dorothy admitted.

'I see.'

It was remarkable how Margot managed to invest those two words with so much disapproval.

'Can we talk about it later?' Dorothy asked, conscious of Jessica only a few yards away in the drawing-room, the door of which she had left ajar.

'Very well. But I certainly think we ought to discuss it.'

'Yes, darling,' Dorothy agreed quietly. 'And the bedroom?'

'Oh, I'll manage in the spare,' Margot replied with that unconvincing off-handedness and rang off again before Dorothy could ask what time she would be arriving.

Jessica was very sweet and understanding when Dorothy told her, insisting that she should move rooms, although Dorothy managed to persuade her finally that it wouldn't be necessary, and full of delight for Dorothy's sake that Margot was coming, although Dorothy herself had reservations. She knew she was in for a difficult time and she was perfectly right.

Margot confronted her with the subject of Jessica soon after she arrived, when Dorothy accompanied her upstairs to help with the unpacking, although there was really no need. Margot had brought lots of books and papers with her but hardly anything in the way of clothes and those she soon bundled away in the wardrobe, refusing Dorothy's offer of help. With nothing to do, Dorothy sat on the bed, hoping Margot would notice the new cover and lamp, the bowl of roses that Jessica had arranged on the dressing-table, but conscious herself of the damp stain over the window and the heavy presence of her daughter in the small room. She had put on weight, Dorothy remarked and thought with self-reproachful objectivity that trousers didn't suit her. They made her look too broad across the bottom. She ought to wear something more loosely cut; one of those long, softly-gathered skirts like Jessica's; so pretty and flattering to the figure. Hands clasped in her lap, she waited for Margot's attack.

It came without any preamble.

'How long exactly does she intend staying?'

'I don't know, darling. Nothing's been decided definitely although I know she'd like to get a job and a place of her own as soon as she can.'

'And meanwhile is she paying you anything towards her keep?'

'Well, not really . . .'

'Oh, Mother, you are hopeless!'

How often had Dorothy heard that exasperated cry? Hopeless about remembering to get the car serviced. Hopeless about refusing to dismiss Meakin, the jobbing gardener, even after he'd been caught taking vegetables to sell in the village. Hopeless about complaining in shops over poor service and shoddy goods.

'But it's all being sorted out,' Dorothy added much too quickly. 'Arthur Bailey – you remember him? – well, he telephoned me the other evening to say he's been in touch with someone at the Brazilian embassy who's going to make inquiries, only he doesn't want Jessica to know about it yet in case nothing comes of it.'

'I thought you said everything had to be sold,' Margot said coldly.

'Yes, it had, but Arthur thinks there's a chance something might be saved; shares, perhaps, or even an annuity from the firm Charlie worked for. After all, he was a director. And then, if there *is* any money . . .'

But Dorothy couldn't continue because then presumably Jessica would go away and the house would be empty once more.

'And if there's nothing?' Margot asked, determinedly practical.

'Well, then we'll have to see what happens,' Dorothy replied, conscious that she sounded much too light-hearted at the prospect. 'But we'll cross that bridge when we come to it.'

The phrase had a nice efficient ring to it that seemed to satisfy Margot who shrugged unwilling acceptance although Dorothy, who rose to her feet and, murmuring something about getting lunch, made her escape, admitted to herself as she went down the stairs that she had never been very good at crossing bridges, preferring to linger happily in cosy familiarity on the near bank.

The next few days passed uncomfortably although Jessica and Dorothy between them made valiant efforts to make Margot's visit pleasant. It was Margot who was difficult, rejecting all their attempts at conversation, with some curt, dismissive comment, refusing offers of outings to Long Barton or even a stroll round the garden.

She went instead for walks by herself or shut herself up in the breakfast room, announcing loudly that she didn't want to be disturbed as she had masses of work to catch up with.

It was with relief that Dorothy heard the doors slam behind her.

For herself, she didn't mind too much. She was used to Margot's abruptness. It was its effect on Jessica that made her anxious. Not that Jessica said anything. She had far too much sensibility to comment but sometimes over meals when they sat together in the dining-room and Margot had refused yet again Jessica's delicate offers of shared companionship, Dorothy saw a shadow pass across the girl's face and a hurt, bewildered look come into her

157

eyes. It was like a child who, having given a grown-up a flower, saw it thrown down on the ground.

It was Margot who criticised and cross-examined.

'What does she do all day?' she asked on one occasion, cornering Dorothy in the greenhouse.

'Oh, she helps me about the house and in the garden,' Dorothy replied defensively. 'She does the shopping sometimes in the village and always shares in the washing-up.'

She tailed off. It seemed pointless to catalogue the little tasks that Jessica performed, especially under Margot's gimlet eye that appeared to imply, without anything being said, that with Meakin looking after the garden and Mrs Hall coming up daily from the village to do the housework, there really wasn't very much left to keep two women fully occupied. Besides, it wasn't what Jessica did that mattered. It was for what she was that Dorothy cherished her.

'Have you heard anything yet from Arthur Bailey?' Margot asked, switching the attack.

She asked the question every day and each time Dorothy had to say no, he hadn't telephoned. Secretly she hoped he wouldn't; not for ages yet, and certainly not until Margot had gone back to London. That way, she would have time to think over quietly the implications of whatever news he had to tell her of Jessica's affairs without Margot rushing her into a decision.

But it wasn't to be. His telephone call came on the last evening of Margot's visit. It was quite late, just after Jessica had offered to go to the kitchen to make bed-time drinks for them all, leaving Dorothy and Margot alone in the drawing-room. Margot was reading one of the thick, dark-covered books on psychology she had brought with her, making heavy marks in the margin and occasionally letting out a snort of impatience as if she disapproved of the author's opinions. Dorothy sat by the window, pretending to read too, but glancing up from the pages at frequent intervals to look beyond her own reflection in the darkened glass to the image of her daughter, seated in the room behind her, and thinking with sad, guilty relief that tomorrow she would be gone and, once more, they had not come any closer together; if anything they were even further apart.

It was then that the telephone rang and, answering it, she heard Arthur Bailey's voice at the other end of the line.

'Dorothy, are you alone?' he asked, sounding worried and flustered, not at all like his usual business-like, pompous self. 'No one can overhear?'

'No,' she replied, bewildered, glancing down the hall. The drawing-room door was shut and the kitchen was too far away for Jessica to hear any of their conversation.

'Well, listen,' he went on urgently. 'That man from the embassy has been in touch with me and I'm afraid things aren't quite what they seem.'

'You mean about the money?' she asked, trying not to sound too pleased. If there was no hope, then . . . But Arthur Bailey was hurrying on.

'No, not just the money, although that comes into it. From what the man told me it seems it wasn't Charlie's fault. It was spent unwisely but not by him. I don't want to be too explicit over the phone but you get my drift?'

She got his drift; got, too, the self-important, conspiratorial note in his voice, too breathy and close to the mouthpiece. Arthur Bailey, although deeply shocked, was enjoying the situation. She felt her hand grasp the telephone receiver so tightly that her knuckles hurt.

'But that's not all,' he continued. 'It seems just before his death, Charlie had been making inquiries about the possibility of a divorce. Then he was found dead in bed. There was even talk at the time that it might have been suicide. He was a very worried man.'

'But . . .' she began.

'Oh, I know,' he interrupted. 'It was a heart attack, brought on no doubt by stress. But I thought you ought to know.'

'Yes, yes,' she heard herself saying, although yes to what she didn't know. Yes to Charlie dying at thirty. Yes to the possibility that Jessica might have been the cause. Yes to the realisation that her relationship with the girl lay in small, glittering pieces like one of those glass Christmas tree balls, once so delicate and pretty, now nothing more than a few, thin, silvery fragments that she hadn't yet the courage or the resolution to decide what to do with.

'And there's no money,' Arthur Bailey was saying with gloomy satisfaction. 'Not a brass farthing. In fact, there's still debts left behind that haven't been settled.'

She didn't answer but stood looking down the hall at the vista of closed doors.

'Dorothy?'

'Yes, I'm here,' she said, rousing herself.

'I suppose I ought to speak to Jessica. Not about anything I've just told you. I think we ought to keep that under our hats, at least for the time being.'

'Under our hats,' she murmured ridiculously in agreement.

'I'll just say I tried to check up on Charlie's affairs and drew a blank. It's best, don't you think? Under the circumstances? Although I must say . . .'

She didn't want to hear what he had to say, knowing he was going to make some moral judgement.

'I'll fetch her,' she said quickly and, putting down the receiver on the table, walked along the hall, trying to arrange her lips into a smile.

'Jessica,' she announced brightly, opening the kitchen door on to a tableau that she knew was significant although she couldn't imagine why; Jessica in the act of turning away from the tray of cups, set out in readiness on the dresser, to throw something in at the open door of the Aga.

'Yes?' Jessica asked and there was a blind look on her face, unfocussed, blank.

'Arthur Bailey's on the phone. He'd like to speak to you.'

For a long moment, their eyes held, Jessica's still with that dazed, unseeing expression.

'You'd better go,' Dorothy said gently, 'I'll see to the tray.'

Their glance broke and Jessica passed her in the doorway without speaking, her head averted, only her profile visible with her lips slightly open as if in a silent gasp.

Crossing the room to close the Aga door, Dorothy noticed something burning on top of the coke; a small, incandescent scrap of paper that blackened and fell apart as she looked at it.

Why did she feel a tight clutch of fear at the sight of it? After all, it was nothing, just rubbish that Jessica had thrown into the fire and yet, as she turned away to pick up the tray, she knew it had something to do with the scene she had walked into; a moment caught in time like a still outside a cinema, implying a whole drama that continued beyond and around the one immobile image.

Jessica had been doing something to the tray at the very moment that Dorothy had opened the door; of that she was convinced, although she had not seen exactly what. She glanced down at it now as she prepared to pick it up. There were three cups placed on it, together with the cream jug and sugar basin and a plate of digestive biscuits; coffee for Jessica and Margot, cocoa for herself because coffee kept her awake if she drank it too late at night. Although cream had not been added, the coffee had been poured out and that was unusual. Normally, the percolator was carried into the drawing-room on the tray and they helped themselves.

Something about the arrangement of the cups struck her, too, as strange. It was much too precise, the cups sets out in a triangle, as if repeating in their positions the places which the three of them occupied in the room, with herself at the apex, as it were, by the window,

Margot to the right of the fireplace, Jessica to the left.

As she picked up the tray, she sharpened her attention to the cups themselves and saw on top of the coffee on the right a faint, whitish scum that was already beginning to dissolve and disappear like the scrap of paper in the Aga.

And then she knew without any doubt what Jessica had intended; knew, too, how Charlie had died; knew why; understood it all. But what she still couldn't understand was how Jessica had hoped to get away with it a second time unless, and the thought struck her like a physical blow, she had counted on Dorothy's affection for her to help her cover up the crime. And, innocent of it, she might have done so, she realised, incapable of believing anything so dreadful about Jessica, thinking it a tragic coincidence and explaining it away by stressing how hard Margot had been working recently and the strain she was put to over her job.

'What's happening about the coffee? Isn't Jessica supposed to be getting it?'

It was Margot, bursting into the kitchen, looking exasperated and deprived at having been kept waiting. Seeing Dorothy standing there with the tray, she added, 'Oh, Mother, you are hopeless. It must be getting cold.'

Yes, I really am hopeless, helpless, incapable, Dorothy thought as she allowed Margot to take the tray from her and put it down on the table, watched her add cream and sugar to the left-hand cup and carry it out of the room.

But not without a certain resolution, she thought, as she moved the remaining cup of coffee over to the left-hand side of the tray before picking it up and following Margot into the hall where Jessica was putting down the telephone receiver.

There had been too much waiting on the bank, she decided. It was time one bridge was crossed for Margot's sake; not that she would ever realise it; for Charlie's too, although in his case, she liked to think of him standing on the far side, holding out his hand to encourage her.

'Your coffee's ready, Jessica,' she announced and even found the courage to smile her thanks as Jessica held the drawing-room door open for her.

Ted Willis

PROOF

Was it simply coincidence that threw the two strangely different young people together, or was some stronger, more malevolent force at work? It is hard to explain such things. If two total strangers should happen to meet twice in the space of an hour or so that might well be dismissed as a coincidence, lucky or otherwise; but if they should, so to speak, accidentally collide with each other no fewer than four times in a short period of time, and if murder should follow as a direct result of their coming together, then perhaps some different explanation must be put forward.

However that may be, there can be no doubt that Edgar Glass considered that it was destiny, working to an ordered plan, which had drawn Margo Webster towards him. He first saw her in the bookshop where he worked, brushed against her quite by accident as he reached up to re-arrange some paperbacks. He stammered a brief apology, aware of cool, sky-blue eyes regarding him without expression. She turned away without responding, leaving behind an impression of Nordic fairness and elegance.

He glanced at her retreating back, his lips pursed, resenting her indifference only for a brief moment. No girl with any remote claim to good looks had ever looked at him with interest and he had grown accustomed to it. He was twenty-eight years of age and his only sexual experiences had been found in the grubby bed of a Soho prostitute. These excursions to the room in Lisle Street were rare, for they left him with an overwhelming sense of disgust and self-contempt. He went only when the ache in his flesh had built up until it became a fever strong enough to consume his shame.

Fifteen minutes later, on the stroke of 12.30, he left the shop for his lunchtime break. Edgar distrusted the food served in restaurants and cafés, and each day, summer and winter, rain or sunshine, he went to the bandstand in the park, taking with him a lunch of sandwiches made with wholemeal bread, and an apple. He ate slowly, chewing each mouthful with care, and then, following his usual routine, he walked from the bandstand to the boating pool, through the ornamental gardens and back round the playing fields to the main gates. He knew, because he had calculated it carefully, that this added up to a distance of just over two miles. He moved with brisk, purposeful strides, head back, taking deep breaths and emptying his lungs slowly. It gave him a feeling of pride to know that he was exercising his body in this regular, disciplined way.

The girl was just entering the park as he reached the gates. He checked without thinking, as though startled. She simply gave him a quick sideways glance and moved on, but he was sure that she had recognised him. Once again, though more strongly than before, he was conscious of the vivid blueness of her eyes. There was no doubt that she was very beautiful. During the afternoon he watched the door of the shop, wondering if she would come back, yet reproaching himself at the same time for such foolishness.

It was 6.30 when he locked up and left the shop, a half-hour later than usual. He hated leaving untidy shelves, and during the course of a busy afternoon some of the customers had upset his neat, alphabetical arrangement of the books. It sometimes occurred to him that people did this sort of thing deliberately; so many of them, especially the young, had no sense of order or discipline.

Later, it was this brief delay that was to convince him that his meeting with Margo was more, much more than coincidence. Had he left at his normal time he would have walked to his home in Wood Green; but that night he was going to the local Evening Institute for the first lesson in a course on Musical Appreciation, and he decided to save time by taking a bus. This in itself was a radical decision, for some two years earlier he had decided, as far as possible, to boycott the public transport system. In his view, the sheer squalor of the trains and buses was not only a national disgrace, but a health hazard of the gravest kind.

To his astonishment, he saw the girl again, sitting towards the front of the bus. He felt his heart quicken, his body tremble with excitement. She sat upright, looking out of the window, and once she raised a hand and rubbed the glass clear of condensation. It seemed to him that she invested even this ordinary movement with an extraordinary grace. Was she aware of his presence, of the intensity of his interest? It seemed possible, for after a few moments she turned and glanced back at him. Once again, her face was without expression. He turned his head away quickly, in confusion, afraid she might think that he was following her deliberately.

She left the bus at the stop before his own, and as she passed his seat, their eyes met. He was certain that there was a hint of a smile on her face, as though she were saying: 'You again.' Then she was gone, hurrying away through the evening drizzle which dripped on the grey streets. He let out a loud, involuntary sigh, causing a man opposite to give him an enquiring look.

Edgar wondered about following her, he could not bear the thought that he might not see her again; but his sense of inferiority, a fear of appearing foolish, held him pinned to his seat. He felt a familiar, urgent stirring of the flesh, and the thought of a visit to Lisle Street flashed into his mind, only to be put sternly aside. It was shameful that he should be so weakminded. To think of a common whore at such a moment was almost a sacrilege.

He was sure now that some purpose was at work in his life, the business had gone beyond coincidence. Yet he was still surprised when he saw her yet again, just over an hour later, at the Evening Institute. He was waiting at the enrolment desk when she came in, shaking the raindrops from an umbrella with a white, transparent cover. Now the compelling blue eyes looked at him directly, studying him, and her face opened up in a full, mischievous smile.

'Well, really,' she said, 'if we go on meeting like this, people will begin to talk.'

He giggled nervously, cursing himself for doing so. Her smile vanished as though at the touch of a switch, and she swept past him, a flicker of contempt in her eyes.

He sat through the class on Musical Appreciation without taking in a single word, without making a single entry in the new notebook he had bought especially for the course. The girl was at another lecture, but he had the extraordinary feeling that she was there with him and within him, that she had taken possession of his mind and body. It was beyond logic or reason and it was beyond experience also, for never in his life had he felt like this. A strange heat seemed to be burning in his blood, he could feel the sweat breaking out like tiny, greasy teardrops on the palms of his hands, on his neck, and soaking into the back of his shirt.

He was in dread of missing her, and somehow, from somewhere, he found the courage to leave the class a few minutes early, braving the stares of the lecturer and the other students, and to wait by the main doors.

She came into the entrance-hall with the tutor, a tall, bearded man in corduroy trousers and check shirt, with a red kerchief knotted at his throat, and stood talking quietly with him for a moment. She glanced towards Edgar almost as though she'd been expecting him to be there. The tutor went off in another direction and she walked across to the doors.

'Is it still raining?' she asked.

'I think – I think it's stopped.' His voice sounded as though it came from another person, he bunched his hands into fists in an effort to stop the trembling of his body. He felt helpless in her presence, like a child waiting tremulously for a kind word, a gesture.

'I wondered if you'd wait,' she said.

'I thought – you know – ' he answered feebly, not knowing what to say.

'I live just off Turnpike Lane. Do you go that way?'

'Yes. I mean – yes.' The lie was quick and eager.

'Then let's walk together, shall we?'

It was as simple as that. When they reached her home, the basement flat of a big, old house, she took out a key, opened the front door and invited him in as though it were the most natural thing in the world. During the walk from the Institute, through the anonymity of the shadowed streets, he had found himself talking with more freedom than for years, but when she switched on the lamps the old, nagging shyness returned. He stood in the doorway, plucking at a button on his raincoat, tongue-tied and awkward. He tried not to look at the large, double divan-bed which, though partly surrounded by a sort of Japanese screen, seemed to dominate the room.

'Come in,' she said briskly. 'Coffee or chocolate?'

'Whatever you're making – '

'Chocolate, then.' There was a touch of asperity in her tone, as though he had irritated her in some way. 'Light the gas-fire. Take your coat off.' She disappeared into the kitchen.

He took off his raincoat and folded it over a chair, lit the fire, and then allowed himself to look at the room in more detail. It was impressively neat and clean, and almost spartan in its furnishing. There was no clutter of ornaments, photographs or indoor plants. A single, graceful stem of copper beech stood in a vase in the white-painted bookshelves, emphasising the simplicity of the surroundings. The raincoat seemed out of place, and he took it out to the small entry-hall. He went back, and sitting on the edge of a chair, began to leaf aimlessly through a book which lay on a low, perspex table.

'Do you know it?' Her voice startled him and he jumped up. 'Do sit down!' she went on sharply, and put two mugs of hot chocolate on the table. 'Do you know that book?'

'No. I don't think I do.'

'You should read it.' She sat on the floor looking up at him, cupping one of the mugs in her hands.

He glanced down at the book, to avoid those eyes, which seemed to be assessing him, stripping him of any defence. '*The Proofs of Love* – it's an interesting title.'

'What the author is saying – in essence – is that every idea and every emotion must be proved in action. It is not enough simply to assert that one has feelings of love or hate. Love and hate are not tangible – they exist only when they are proved by deeds. When a man says that he loves a certain cause or a certain person – he must be prepared to put that statement to the test, to kill even – or be killed – to prove his sincerity. Such a man would be a super-being, marked out from the common herd. It's an interesting concept, don't you think?'

He was drawn back once more to her eyes, as though mesmerised. She had spoken calmly, in a matter-of-fact tone, but for some reason the words chilled him and he felt suddenly afraid. One of his legs began to tremble, and he put a hand on his knee to stop the shaking. He had an extraordinary feeling of unreality, as if all this were happening to another person.

Without waiting for him to answer, she added another question. 'Do you live alone?'

'With my mother. She's a widow.'

'Do you love her?'

'It's not – it's not something I've thought about.'

169

Fumbling nervously, he drew a packet of cigarettes from his pocket. She raised her eyebrows a little and he said quickly: 'Do you mind?'

'Is it important to you?'

'Not really. I ration myself strictly – five each day.'

'If it isn't important, why don't you give it up?'

'I keep saying I will – but I never get round to it.'

'Give me the cigarettes,' she said, holding out a hand. He gave them to her meekly, and she set them down on the table. 'We'll leave them there. And we shall see who is the stronger : you – or a few cigarettes.'

They sat in silence for a few moments, sipping the chocolate. At length he plucked up enough courage to ask tentatively, 'What do you do? I mean, your job?'

'I'm a teacher,' she said. 'Or rather, I was.'

'You're not working?'

'Not at present. I was teaching in the Midlands.'

'Why did you leave?'

'I didn't. I was fired. They didn't like my methods, or my ideas. I tried to teach standards, values, discipline – and that didn't go down well with our progressive head-master.' She weighted the last two words with sarcasm.

'I wish more teachers felt like you!' he said boldly, as though she had touched some secret spring inside him, releasing feelings that he had never before put into words. 'You should see some of the louts we get in the bookshop sometimes – call themselves students – long-haired, in-solent, filthy jeans, dirty suede boots – ugh. When I think that they're supposed to be the future of this country. If I had my way –'

'What would you do?'

'Put them into a Labour Corps, make them do some real work. That's what they need – work and discipline.'

'It's what the whole country needs,' she said softly, and added, 'You are a man of firm opinions. I like that.'

Flattered by her praise, he said airily, 'Oh, I have my views. A lot of people don't think so, because I keep them to myself. I watch and listen. But one day, I'll speak out, they'll see a different side of me!'

Was it really him saying all this, talking now with such confidence? Somehow this woman seemed to have the power to make him react like a child one moment, a man the next. Her look of approval sent a feeling of power and masculine authority surging through him and he sat back in the chair for the first time.

She took up a cigarette, and in his new relaxed role, he wagged a finger and said, 'Ah! Who is being weak now?'

'The difference is, that I can take it or leave it. I am in control, not the cigarette,' she said coolly. 'Light, please.'

He struck a match for her. She sucked on the cigarette, and blew a plume of smoke into the air, mocking him. And then, quite suddenly, she said: 'Are you a virgin?'

'No.' He felt his cheeks redden, and to cover the embarrassment he added, with greater emphasis, 'Of course not!'

She nodded, her eyes holding his, and held out the glowing cigarette. 'Do you want this?'

'No.'

She put a hand on the inside of his leg, and he sat forward, his flesh screaming. 'But you want me, don't you?' He could only stare at her, and she increased the pressure on his leg. 'Don't you, Edgar?'

He reached out for her desperately, but she eluded his grasp, and pointed the cigarette at him. 'Put it out for me.' He took up an ashtray, and she said sharply, 'No. Not there!'

She took his hand and turned the palm upwards. The irises of her eyes seemed to have darkened, to have grown bigger, her body had tensed, and the tip of her tongue showed through parted lips.

'Pain and love,' she said, 'aren't they the same thing, two sides of one coin? Pain can be a proof of love, isn't that true?'

She lowered the cigarette towards his palm, her eyes boring into his. He sat without moving, the sense of unreality stronger than ever; but when the burning red tobacco touched his skin he cried out in pain, and pulled his hand away. Her lips curled in contempt and before he could check her she pressed the cigarette into her own palm. He cried out again, and pulled her hands apart. Looking down in horror at the scorched flesh, he pressed his lips against the burn.

She gave a strange, rather high-pitched humourless laugh, put up her free arm and pulled him down to her.

There were many times in the next few months when Edgar woke with the sweat of fear on his body. It was always in his own bed, for Margo would never allow him to stay the whole night. When he begged to be allowed to do so, or spoke of going away together – even of marriage – she either laughed in his face or changed the subject. For weeks on end she would remain placid and reserved, loving him gently though somehow at a distance, without passion, as though her thoughts were elsewhere : and then, for brief periods, she would become, so to speak, another person, wild, unpredictable, restless, terrifying.

She had not yet secured a regular job, but had begun to give private tuition to a few young people. One evening he found her going over some examination papers with one of her pupils, a shy, pretty girl of fifteen named Lucy, who already looked like a young woman. Margo appeared to be calm and relaxed. She greeted Edgar with a light kiss, introduced him to the girl, and went to the kitchen to make some coffee.

Once Lucy got over her initial shyness, she talked quite freely. It was clear that she looked upon Margo with feelings which were a mixture of awe and admiration. Over the coffee they spoke amiably of school and examinations, with Margo largely silent, watching them with a fixed smile. At last, the girl got up to leave.

'I must go, miss, Mother will be expecting me.'

'You look very pretty today, Lucy. I love the skirt,' said Margo. 'Here, let me see.'

The girl moved closer, and Margo ran her fingers down the side of the skirt, smoothing the material over the girl's thigh in a gesture which was almost a caress. 'Beautiful!' she said.

'I made it myself,' said Lucy.

Margo stood up and circled the girl, smiling. 'You are lovely, Lucy, do you know that? Would you believe she is only fifteen, Edgar? With such a figure!'

As usual, he could only stare, knowing that Margo was on the edge of one of her moods, his flesh tingling with that strange mixture of anticipation, excitement and fear which she seemed able to induce in him at will.

'I've an idea, Edgar,' said Margo. 'Why don't we keep Lucy here, as our prisoner? Yes! That's it! We won't let her go. She shall be our slave, to do our bidding!' She took the girl's chin in her long, graceful fingers. 'Would you like that, Lucy? Would you like to stay? You will have to be good, of course, willing and submissive. Edgar can be very strict, he believes in discipline. But if you are good — well, he can be very kind also.'

The girl simply stood there, her breasts rising and falling under the white blouse, unable to move, unable to tear herself away from the spell cast by those intense blue eyes. And then, with the same swift change of mood with which she had begun the scene, Margo stepped back.

'Right. Joke over! Away you go then or your mother will be worrying about you. I'll see you tomorrow evening, at the same time.'

The girl gathered her things, stammered a farewell, and hurried away. Margo went into the hall with her and he heard them whispering together. The front door closed and Margo came back. She looked at Edgar, her face set in an odd, questioning smile. 'Do you fancy her?'

'She's a child!'

'Would you like me to arrange it?' She laughed. 'I could, you know.'

He moved towards her. 'I want you.'

'No!' she said mockingly, 'Oh, no!'

'Margo –'

'No! You bore me, sicken me. You'd better go. Yes. Go away.'

'Margo – what's wrong?'

'I mean it. I am not going to bed with you any more, Edgar. I can manage without it, you will have to do the same.' Once, regretting it afterwards, he had told her about his visits to Soho, and now she salted the wound. 'You can always go back to your favourite whore!'

She picked up the tray with the empty coffee cups and went into the kitchen. He hurried after her, as though drawn by a string.

'Margo – it can't – we can't finish like this!'

'I didn't say it was finished. I simply said that I wouldn't sleep with you again.'

'Why? Why? What have I done?'

'You've done nothing. Nothing! That's the trouble. Sex makes you satisfied, complacent, I can see that now. And dull, so dull that I could scream.'

'What is it you want – what is it?' His voice rose to a scream of desperation.

She turned to him, her voice low, her eyes glittering like ovals of blue ice. 'You say you love me.'

'I do.'

'I want proof. I want more than words. I want proof, Edgar.'

He touched her arm and the flesh was as cold as her eyes. She moved away from him and went back to the sitting room. He held on to the sink, head forward, eyes closed. He was a child again, remembering the times, the countless times, when after some small infringement of the household rules laid down by his father he had been locked in the cellar under the stairs to await punishment. Often he had stayed in the darkness for hours, fear feeding on his imagination. Through the crack in the door he would sometimes hear his mother plead with his father, but there was no escape. Sooner or later, the bolt would be drawn, the door opened and he would be summoned forth. He felt as though he were in that cellar now, locked into a sequence of events which possessed their own inevitability, and from which, as before, there was no escape.

He heard music and lifted his head. With a long sigh, he gathered himself and went into the other room. Margo was sitting cross-legged on the floor beside the record-player, and his spirits rose like a man reprieved, as she smiled and patted the floor beside her, indicating that he should join her.

'Do you know this music?' she asked.

'Wagner?'

'Yes. Wagner. *Rheingold.*'

She closed her eyes and put back her head. The flaxen hair seemed to float over her shoulders, the light of the single lamp not only drew out and enhanced the smooth beauty of her face, but added a sort of radiance, an innocence, that overwhelmed him. He touched her cheek with his fingers, and took her hand, as though afraid that she might vanish. The skin was still cold, but she did not repulse him.

'I couldn't leave you,' he whispered, 'I could never leave you. I haven't the strength.'

She spoke as though she hadn't heard him. '*Rheingold.* Valhalla – the home of the Gods. But even Valhalla had to be paid for. Do you remember? The price was Freia, the Goddess of Youth.'

Once again, he felt his flesh prickle with apprehension, but with excitement also. 'Tell me what you want – tell me what to do.' His voice crackled and trembled.

'Don't you know?'

'Tell me.'

'Do you truly love me?'

'Yes, yes, yes!'

'And if I ask for proof?'

'Anything!'

She turned her face towards him. Her voice seemed to come from out of a mist. 'Would you kill, take a human life?'

'Yes. If you asked me.'

'Kill?'

'Kill.'

It was her turn to sigh now, a sigh that seemed to force itself from her body, as though she were expelling some oppressive spirit. She opened the fingers of his hand and touched the palm with her tongue, looking into his eyes as she did so. 'Wait,' she said.

She rose, went to a drawer, and came back to him with a piece of shining black cloth, which she placed on the floor between them. Smiling, watching his face, she turned back the cloth to reveal a knife, a sheathed dagger with a swastika and a death's head symbol on the handle. She drew out the shining blade.

'A souvenir of the war,' she said. 'I bought it in Amsterdam ten years ago. Isn't it beautiful?' He nodded. 'Give me your hand.'

Like a man in a trance he extended a hand and she pricked the ball of his thumb with the point of the knife. He tightened his lips, but made no sound. She cut herself in the same way and pressed her bloodied thumb against his.

'As it was in the book,' she whispered. 'Joined in blood. A True Couple.' She dropped the knife and pulled him over on to her with animal fierceness, sinking her teeth into his neck so that he cried out with pain and ecstasy. But when he plucked at her clothing, she rolled aside and got to her feet. 'No. Not yet!' she said. 'First, your promise. The proof.' She picked up the knife. 'Lucy will be back soon.'

'Lucy – but you said – '

'I asked her to run an errand before she went home. I sent her to buy a bottle of wine.' He saw again that her eyes seemed to be enlarged, the irises darker, and she was trembling as with excitement. She stooped and picked up the knife, holding the handle towards him. 'Lucy. Young and lovely. Our Freia. The Goddess of Youth.'

Her voice, deep and husky, seemed to come not from her body, but some distant place. He knew now that she was ill, sick to the point of madness; and he felt that he, too, was caught up in that same madness, drawing from it a strange and terrible strength. His fingers closed around the knife.

She went to the record-player, and started the same record as before. As the music poured forth, she smiled and turned to him.

'Do you feel as I do?' she whispered. He nodded. 'Like the moment before a great storm, when the air presses on your skin. Or driving at great speed – Oh, Edgar, my darling, I love you.' She came to him and kissed his lips, his eyes, his forehead as though bestowing a blessing. 'You understand why you must do it?'

'Yes,' he whispered.

'The ultimate proof.'

'Yes.'

'Afterwards – afterwards we shall be together always.'

The doorbell rang shrilly, startling him so much that the knife fell from his hand. All the strength which had possessed him only a moment before seemed to drain from his body. He looked at her, limp and fearful.

'What's the matter?' she asked sharply.

'I can't.'

'Pick up the knife!'

'I can't, Margo. Not now, not tonight.'

'Tonight! It has to be tonight.'

'No!' The word came out like a scream.

She stared at him. 'I thought I'd changed you. I thought I'd made you strong. But you're weak, weak and contemptible. Look at you! You stand there like a whipped dog, looking at me with those weak, watery eyes. You disgust me, you know that?'

He heard a sound like a whip-lash in his head, heard it echo in his brain, as though some link had snapped, and he seemed suddenly to be surrounded by a swirling red mist. Within that mist, he felt himself reach down for the knife, felt her hair in his clenched fingers, felt the blade thrust into a great softness, again and again and again, felt a gushing warmth on his face and hand as the red mist deepened to crimson.

From somewhere beyond, from another world perhaps, there came the insistent ringing of a bell, cutting across the music.

Jacqueline Wilson

THE BOY WHO COULDN'T READ

Mr Croft worked the children hard for most of the day. He believed in getting straight down to it, first day of term or not. But he'd relented by the last lesson. He was a little worried by their sullen obedience. They gathered round the other teachers in the playground and laughed and chatted without any inhibitions but no one ever came and talked to him now. Perhaps he was too hard on them?

He decided to give them a little treat. He'd read to them for twenty minutes and then let them draw a picture. He fumbled in the back of the cupboard and found his old copy of *The Mountain of Adventure*. You couldn't beat a good Enid Blyton adventure story, no matter what all these trendy educationalists said. Let them read obscure fantasies or sordid kiddie kitchen sink. He knew what the children liked.

But one child didn't like *The Mountain of Adventure*. Mr Croft looked up after a couple of pages and saw David Bates hunched up over his own book. He stopped reading aloud and the children held their breath. It took David a few seconds before he noticed the expectant silence.

'What are you doing, David Bates?'

'I'm sorry,' said David, snapping his book shut.

'Let me see that.'

David sighed and handed the book over. It was a book on astronomy. Mr Croft thumbed through it and then gave it back.

'Why were you looking at that instead of listening to the story?'

'I – I'm interested in astronomy.'

'Oh yes? And I take it you're not interested in *The Mountain of Adventure*?'

'Not really.'

'Why, may I ask?'

'Well, I think it's a bit infantile, if you really want to know.'

Someone tittered.

'Infantile. Oh, I see. The boy wonder prefers to read an adult book on astronomy, correct?'

'Yes.'

'What tosh! You silly little boy. We all know you can't even read properly. Of course you can't manage to read that astronomy book, you're just showing off.'

'I can read it,' said David, his face getting red.

'I've heard you read, boy. You have to have your special coaching, don't you?'

'I *can* read.'

'Very well. Demonstrate. Come out to the front of the class. You're always trying to tell me my job. Well, you take over altogether. Here's *The Mountain of Adventure.* Very infantile, right? Well, read it then. Read it out loud to the class.'

David stood up, burning. He took the book and cleared his throat. He read, stumbling, hesitating, with little expression. Another child giggled nervously, but most were still and silent, their own faces red.

'That's enough, lad. A five-year-old could do better,' said Mr Croft. 'You can hardly read at all. Sit down then.'

Mr Croft read on to the end of the chapter. David Bates sat motionless throughout. Then Mr Croft handed round pieces of paper and told the children to do a drawing to illustrate the story. There were only ten minutes left of the lesson but they passed very slowly. The bell rang at last and the children stretched and sighed. One stood up, several disappeared behind their desk lids.

Mr Croft rapped on his own desk with the blackboard eraser.

'What are you doing? I didn't say that the lesson is over,' he said, although he had also sagged with relief. He decided he was too exhausted to make an issue of it. It was the first day of term after all. They always took a few days to simmer down, especially after Christmas.

'Very well. Off you go,' he said, in a kindlier fashion. 'Hand in your drawings as you go.'

They handed in their efforts. Some were hastily scribbled and coloured with school wax crayon. Others were lovingly embellished with privately owned felt-tip pen. Gideon Symons handed in a masterpiece worthy of a gold star, his artistic ability enormously aided by his huge tin of forty Caran D'Ache.

David Bates passed Mr Croft's desk without pausing.

'David?'

The child's face was still unusually red but he maintained his irritating composure.

'Yes, Mr Croft?'

'Hand in your drawing, David.'

'There's little point,' said David, and he handed in a blank sheet of paper. He waited.

Mr Croft looked at the blank paper, wanting to crumple it.

'I suppose you think you're being clever,' he said eventually.

David chose not to reply. Mr Croft looked at his peaky face and spiky hair and round spectacles. A sparrow of a child with owl eyes. There'd been other kids equally bright. Disturbing kids. Kids who wet themselves or couldn't sit still or had epileptic fits on the woodblock floor. Kids with nits, kids with knives. Kids like Gideon Symons with his Caran D'Ache crayons and his yellow Kickers boots. All sorts of kids, but he'd never hated one the way he hated David Bates.

181

It was hard keeping the hatred out of his voice.

'You're being very silly, David. Now take your paper, go back to your desk, and do me a drawing.'

The few remaining children raised their eyebrows and nudged each other. Mr Croft glared at them and they whisked out of the classroom. David looked at the door, swinging open. For a moment Mr Croft thought he was going to ignore him and walk straight out after them. But David merely sighed elaborately and did as he was told. At least, he took the sheet of paper and sat down at his desk. He did not draw.

'Come along, lad. Get on with it,' said Mr Croft.

David did nothing.

Mr Croft decided to ignore him for five minutes. He picked up his briefcase and took out the compositions 2A had written that morning.

' "What I did at Christmas". Everyone must fill at least two sides of paper. Neat writing, don't forget punctuation and watch that spelling.'

Well, what did they do over Christmas? He gave the first few a glance.

'Mum let me stay up to see Morecambe and Wise it was smashing.'

'My mum and dad and my aunties and uncles all had a few and got ever so tiddly and my Auntie Vi did a can-can and we did have a laugh.'

'I didn't get what I wanted. I really wanted a poodle nightdress case. I got lovely presents and Mum and Dad gave me a Bionic Woman but I really did want a poodle nightdress case.'

Mr Croft leafed through the compositions until he found David's. It was untidy and hopelessly misspelt. He tried to follow the general gist but it became impossible. He wanted to put a savage red line through the incomprehensible essay, but Maple, the headmaster, insisted that David had to be handled sensitively. Mr Croft wondered what Maple would say if he got to hear about this afternoon's little contretemps and his armpits prickled with anxiety. Reluctantly he picked out a handful of mis-spelt words in David's composition and wrote out the correct spellings, leaving space for David to copy each word ten times. Dyslexia! Once upon a time if a kid couldn't read properly by the time it was nearly nine it was thick and that was that. Well, all right, David Bates was no fool, although he wasn't necessarily another Einstein. His Stanford Binet assessment might be up in the 160s, but that only meant he was good at puzzles. That was all these I.Q. tests really were when you got down to it. And what was the use of being able to do silly puzzles when you could barely write your own name?

He glanced at the child. David returned his stare calmly. The piece of paper was still blank.

'I've just about had enough of this behaviour, Bates. Now get drawing. Go on, do as you're told.'

David remained motionless.

'Pick up that pencil and *draw*!'

Mr Croft marched to the desk and wrapped the child's small cold hand round the pencil.

'Now draw,' he said, giving him a hard prod in the back.

David leant on one elbow and let the pencil slide out of his hand back on to the desk.

'I'm warning you, Bates,' said Mr Croft. 'Stop this silly act. You're not impressing me at all. Just get on with your drawing, do you hear?' He waited. '*Pick up that pencil!*'

David jumped but didn't obey. Mr Croft wanted to hit the boy so badly that he went back to his own desk, scared of losing control altogether. David watched him, his small face impassive.

'All right,' said Mr Croft. 'You want to play silly games, we'll play silly games. We shall sit it out. You are not leaving this classroom until you have done me a draw-ing. Do you understand? We shall sit here until breakfast if necessary.'

'Then may I phone my mother?' David asked.

'No, you may not.'

'But she will be worried about me. She always worries if I'm late. It isn't very fair on her,' said David reasonably.

'I'm afraid I can't help that. It's you choosing to worry her, laddie, not me. Do me a drawing and you can be home in no time.'

'Why do you want me to do a drawing so badly?' said David.

'Don't be so damn impertinent! Just remember who you are. You're not here to ask clever-dick questions. You're here to do as you're told. Now *do* as you're told.'

Mr Croft longed to loosen his tie. His shirt was sticking to him. The central heating was turned up ridiculously high. He went to open a few windows. He had to use the window pole, although his hands were shaking badly so that the pole nudged uselessly against the glass many times before connecting. But he persevered, determined not to be defeated.

And he wasn't going to let this supercilious little twerp defeat him either. There wouldn't have been any problem in the old days. One swish of the cane and there wouldn't be any further argument. Not that he was one of these sadistic perverts getting some kind of kick out of caning kiddies. The cane had grown dusty in the cupboard, its very presence serving enough purpose.

He was sure he'd been popular with children then. The boys looked up to him and the little girls had all giggled at his jokes. They'd called him Sir and opened the door for him and worked hard. But now that some of their own children were at the school things were very different. 2A were a lost cause anyway after Jeff Priestly's influence. They spent a whole year in his form without learning how to write a decent sentence or any of their times tables. All they seemed to do was mess around with egg-boxes and toilet rolls. It seemed modern education was literally a load of old rubbish.

But it was no use complaining any more. Jeff Priestly

was well in with Maple, thought to be a fine teacher, for God's sake. What sort of influence was he on the kids, with his shoulder-length hair and his tattered jeans and his cock-eyed Marxist theories? He wasn't even clean: he'd obviously been wearing that ridiculous Cambridge University sweatshirt for days. Cambridge University! Jeff Priestly was probably lucky to scrape five O-levels. Yet the way things were going he'd probably end up a headmaster. He wouldn't stay an underpaid and unappreciated junior school teacher.

But even Jeff Priestly had had a bit of bother with David Bates.

'He's the sort of kid who gets up my nose,' he'd said once in the staff room, in his usual unprepossessing way. 'He seems to have been born middle-aged. He's got this way of peering through his specs at you like a little professor.'

David was peering through his glasses now, arms folded.

'You're obviously intending to spend the night here, my boy,' said Mr Croft. 'Well, it's no skin off my nose. I've got a lot of work here to be getting on with. I'm in no hurry to get home.'

He pretended to mark the children's compositions. He wasn't really bluffing. The Christmas holidays seemed to have gone on for ever, a horrible reminder that this was what it was going to be like all the time when he retired. Only another year and two terms to go.

He hadn't thought he'd mind when Elaine finally moved out. They'd never really got on well together. He thought it would be a relief to be free of her whining. But the house was unpleasantly silent nowadays and although he kept it reasonably clean there was a dead atmosphere to the place, as if it had been sealed up for years.

"What I did at Christmas." Mr Croft had cooked his small oven-ready chicken and his mini Christmas pudding, but halfway through his meal he'd pushed his plate away, put his head down on the checked tablecloth, and wept.

He found his eyes were stinging now and he blinked quickly, horrified. Perhaps he was going to pieces, heading for a breakdown? No, he was just feeling a bit seedy, that was all. Perhaps he was starting 'flu, there was a bug going around at the moment. Maybe that was why he was so hot.

He loosened his tie after all and yawned several times. He was tired too, of course. He hadn't been sleeping well. He'd spent most of last night tossing about under his Marks and Spencer duvet, the double bed growing larger and more lonely by the minute. At least you could tuck yourself in tightly with good old-fashioned sheets and blankets. He'd tried wrapping the duvet round him until he felt like a giant Swiss roll but it still didn't help him to sleep. He'd grown so used to Elaine's warm brushed nylon bulk that he'd lost the knack of sleeping without her.

Funny how you could miss a woman you didn't even like. He hadn't thought much of her right from the start. A silly little shopgirl with painted lips, not his sort at all. She was all right for a bit of messing about, but that was all. Messing about was an accurate description too. Elaine might sport a blonde rinse and lipstick but she knew as little about sex as he did. It was a wonder their Betty ever managed to get herself conceived, her parents' coupling was so brief and inadequate.

Betty had been another disappointment. She'd appalled him as a red-faced shrieking baby, but she'd been an enchanting little girl, with her mother's fluffy good looks and a quick wit that took him by surprise. He had her whizzing through the Beacon Readers by the time she was four. She was top of the class all the way up her junior school and passed to the grammar without any bother. When she was twelve she was on Junior Criss Cross Quiz and did very well for herself too. But everything went wrong when she reached puberty. She wouldn't do her homework, went out dancing, sat around coffee bars. Her mother all over again. He tried pleading with her, slapping her, even locking her out of the house, but she wouldn't see reason.

She was three months pregnant when she took her O-levels. She only passed Domestic Science and Art and didn't seem to give a damn, because she had a wedding ring safe on her finger now. His Betty, swollen with the child of a greasy little garage mechanic who'd been in the lowest stream of a tough Secondary Modern.

The marriage had lasted, much to his surprise, and Betty's husband had his own garage now. Elaine had gone to live with them in their four bedroomed neo-Georgian house on a posh new estate in Surrey. Betty had tried to keep in touch. She'd even invited him for Christmas too, not wanting to appear to take sides, but he wasn't having any.

'Can we come in and do you now?'

Mr Croft looked round, startled. It was a couple of cleaning women, looking impatient.

'We've left you till last, you know. We really ought to be off now.'

David sat up properly. Oh no, you little bugger, thought Mr Croft, I'm not giving up yet.

'I'm afraid you'll have to give this classroom a miss this afternoon, ladies,' he said, in his most authoritative tones.

They tutted a little but went off with their brushes and brooms. The school was very still. It began to get much colder. The heating had obviously gone off for the night. David started shivering. Mr Croft was cold too now, but he decided to put up with his own discomfort.

'We seem to be the only ones left in the school,' he said. 'What a silly boy you are, Bates. Isn't it time you came to your senses?'

David said nothing.

Mr Croft said nothing.

They stared at each other and then both started when

they heard the door slam at the end of the corridor. Maple's door. Oh God, he'd forgotten Maple.

David's eyes glinted behind his glasses. There was going to be hell to pay with Maple. He was never keen on any kind of punishment. He hated the idea of children being kept after class. And it would be a hundred times worse because it was his precious David Bates.

There had been a bit of a barney last term. Mr Croft had made a slip when he was chalking some arithmetic on the board and David Bates immediately pointed out the mistake. He did it in such an offensive way, sighing heavily, eyebrows raised, that Mr Croft couldn't let it go at that. So he blustered, pretending that the mistake had been deliberate. He thought he sounded reasonably convincing, but David Bates gave a tight smile of contempt. Mr Croft sent the boy out of the room for insolence. Maple was indulging in one of his little tours of inspection and found the kid stuck outside the classroom.

Maple was angry but he handled it tactfully enough, saying nothing in front of the children. He waited and had a little chat with Mr Croft after school was over.

'Please don't think I'm interfering, Arthur,' he said, taking pains to sound matey. 'I know just how tiresome these gifted children can be. Maybe I'd have done the same myself. But I don't feel it's quite the right way of coping with the situation. Young David's a highly sensitive child and he needs careful handling. He got off to a very bad start at that other school. His mother assures me he could read fluently before he went to school, but when they started messing him about, insisting he start at the Look, Janet, Look stage, and in i.t.a. too, it confused and frustrated him so much that he became mildly dyslexic. Thank heavens we seem to be winning through. His reading age is only slightly below par now, and when he gets a bit of confidence I'm sure he'll make even greater progress. Can't you see why he badly needs to show off a bit in the lessons he's good at? If I were you I'd praise him as much as possible, Arthur. Thank God we've got rid of the poisonous gold star and form prize competitive clap-trap, but kids still need a pat on the back at times.'

Mr Croft shook his head and nodded at the appropriate moments because he had no other choice, but inwardly he burned with resentment. Maple thought he knew it all because he'd done a course in child psychology but he knew nothing. The kids had liked getting their gold stars for good work. When there weren't any more stars they stopped working. It was as simple as that. And mollycoddling insolent little sods like David Bates made them cockier than ever.

Mr Croft remembered his own schooldays. Miss Jennings at his little village school had been a wonderful woman, but she was a stickler for discipline. The tinies had to sit with their hands on their heads if they were naughty, and the older children got a stinging slap on the back of their legs if they dared get up to mischief. No one would have dreamed of pointing out a mistake to Miss Jennings.

Mr Croft had been a polite little boy, neat and well-scrubbed, his hair smarmed oilily into submission. He had been top of the school and Miss Jennings' favourite. He'd sat the scholarship and passed to the big boys' Grammar in the town.

'You're destined to go far, my boy,' Miss Jennings said, but she had been wrong. Mr Croft had expected to be top of the big boys' Grammar school too but to his shame and horror he was nearer the bottom of the form. He didn't give up. He worked even harder. He passed his school certificate and stayed on in the sixth form and spent every spare minute studying, but it wasn't enough. Boys like David Bates hardly worked at all but they got their scholarships to Oxford and Cambridge. Mr Croft didn't manage university at all. He did well enough at his Teacher Training College and after a while he thought he'd got over his disappointment. He decided to make a go of things and end up a headmaster, but it hadn't worked out that way.

Now he was only hanging on to his job by the skin of his teeth. Maple had already made a few hints about an early retirement. Oh God, this was the very opportunity Maple was looking for.

Mr Croft clenched his fists, waiting for the soft pad of Maple's Hush Puppies along the corridor, come to see why there was still a light in 2A long after everyone else had gone home.

But he didn't come. He couldn't have spotted the light. They heard him go outside, the slam of his car door, the splutter of his ignition key. They heard him drive away.

'Draw me a picture, David,' said Mr Croft.

'I'm not going to,' said David, and for the first time he sounded childish and defiant. 'I'm going home.'

He stood up but Mr Croft was by his side in an instant. 'Sit down again. At once!'

'You can't keep me here by force,' said David, but he didn't sound sure. Mr Croft wasn't a very big man but David was small and slight for his age.

'Draw, David.' Mr Croft put his face very close to the child's. Their breaths mingled. '*Draw!*'

David's face crumpled. He bit his lips, fighting for control, but tears spilled behind his glasses.

'Aah! Poor little diddums,' said Mr Croft.

'You shut up!' David sobbed furiously.

'Don't use that tone with me.'

'You keep making these threats but you can't do anything,' David said. 'I'm going home now. My mother will be ever so worried.'

'Poor little Mumsie's crybaby, eh?'

'You're mad. You're a real nutcase,' David shouted, and he made a run for it.

Mr Croft caught him at the classroom door. David struggled and kicked but Mr Croft had his spindly arms in a pincer grip. David's feet barely touched the ground as Mr Croft pulled him back to his desk. He pushed him down so hard that the child's head juddered with shock.

'There! Now draw, you little runt, draw!'

'I can't! I don't know what to draw,' David wailed.

'Every other child in the class drew me a picture, David Bates. I told them to draw me a scene from *The Mountain of Adventure*. That's what you're going to do, boy. You're no different from the others. You're not getting preferential treatment from me. You're going to draw, do you understand?' He was shouting, spittle shining on his chin.

'But I wasn't – I didn't listen to it,' David sobbed. 'I don't know what it's about. You know I wasn't listening. I *can't* draw.'

'Can't even draw, eh? Can't read. Can't write. Now it turns out the boy wonder can't even draw. Well, you'd better learn fast,' said Mr Croft, 'I'm going to count to five, David Bates. One. Two. Three. Four.'

David picked up the pencil. He drew one jagged uncontrolled line and the lead broke.

'You did that on purpose!' Mr Croft shouted, and he slapped the boy hard across the face.

Mr Croft had caned children in the past. He'd prodded them and pulled them, he'd thrown blackboard chalk at them and rapped their knuckles with his ruler. But he'd never once struck a child across the face. His hand was trembling, wanting to hit again and again. He clenched it, panting.

'Find another pencil,' he said, his voice high-pitched.

David fumbled in his satchel, whimpering, his nose running into his mouth.

'I – I haven't got one.'

Mr Croft felt in his breast pocket for his own ballpoint pen.

'Use this then. Draw with it, draw, draw, *draw*.'

Sudden pain flared in his chest. Mr Croft stared at the child and then doubled up. Red-hot agony. Chest, arm, everywhere. He couldn't draw breath. Couldn't talk. Christ Almighty, the pain.

He swayed in front of David, still holding the ballpoint pen.

'Help! Get help! I'm ill! I'm having a heart attack!' he screamed, but he could only gurgle and drool in the grip of the pain. He clutched the pen and stabbed at the piece of drawing paper.

'P-h-o-n-e 999,' he scrawled desperately. *'Heart.'*

David Bates looked at the piece of paper and then he looked at Mr Croft.

'I can't read, can I?' he said.

Mr Croft slumped to his knees. David walked round him, crumpling the paper and stuffing it into his pocket. He switched off the light, walked along the corridor and out of the silent school.

He met his mother hurrying along the road.

'David, where on earth have you been? I've been so worried.'

'Sorry, Mum. That hateful Croft man kept me in again.'

'This is getting ridiculous. I think I'd better go and see him, David. Come on, we'll go back to the school and have it out with him.'

'No, he'll have gone by now,' David said quickly. 'Don't fuss, Mum. Things will work out. You'll see.'

David tucked his hand in her arm and they went straight home.